WILDE

Eloise always wanted to grow up to be a witch, but she grew up to be a writer instead. She lives by the sea in very west Wales with her artist husband Guy and her opinionated dog, Watson Jones. When she isn't writing stories, she likes walking through storms, smelling blue flowers, unexpected singing, gazing at stars and learning about unusually shaped creatures. She believes we are all made of stories.

Eloise Williams is Children's Laureate Wales (2019-2021). Children's Laureate Wales is a national ambassadorial post which aims to engage and inspire the children of Wales through literature, and to promote every child's right to have their stories and voices heard. The initiative is run by Literature Wales

www.childrenslaureate.wales

WILDE

Eloise Williams

Firefly

First published in 2020
by Firefly Press
25 Gabalfa Road, Llandaff North, Cardiff, CF14 2JJ
www.fireflypress.co.uk

A CIP catalogue record of this book is available from
the British Library.

3 5 7 9 10 8 6 4 2

ISBN 9781913102180
ebook ISBN 9781913102197

*This book has been published with the support of
the Welsh Books Council.*

Typeset by Elaine Sharples

Printed and bound by CPI Group (UK) Ltd, Croydon, CR0 4YY

For Carol, a true individual.

'Be yourself; everyone else is already taken.'
Oscar Wilde

'Though she be but little, she is fierce.'
William Shakespeare

1

Yes, I got kicked out of school on purpose. No, I did not want to be sent to Witch Point.

I thought I'd be sent home, but Dad can't get out of his work in America, so I have to stay with his sister Mae. I'm not speaking to him. I don't think he's speaking to me. I've never been to Mae's house before, because Dad has never let me, and I don't want to go there now. Witch Point is legendary for all the wrong reasons. I wanted to get away from all the weird things that were happening to me and have ended up in the weirdest place in the world.

It's not so bad to look at. The sky is the brightest blue and the fields are a warm, happy yellow. A heatwave in Wales. That's how weird things have got. Extra strange because it was raining and not hot at all where I got on the train and it's only a couple of hours away. I can't wait to go travelling like my dad does. Today I would go to Alaska and cover myself with snow. Closing my eyes against the blistering glare I remember that the world is a very big place and one day I'm going to see lots of it. I force myself off the train. The carriages judder and hiss, then pull away towards freedom. Standing back, I am fried like an egg by the sun.

I find a spot in the shade and try to think calm thoughts. I'm so thirsty, my mouth tastes disgusting: like chewing a dirty sock.

There's a noise just above my head and, squinting up, I see an owl staring down at me from the top of the Witch Point station sign. It spins its head around 360 degrees. It should be asleep in the day. Here we go again.

Birds follow me; I don't know why. They just do. When I look up again, it's been joined by a jackdaw and a crow.

No. Go away. Leave me alone. I'm not going to be weird here. I'm going to be Normal.

I look again and they have vanished. Good.

I worry a lot as I wait. Perhaps Mae has forgotten about me? Or she doesn't want me to stay with her after all? I pace the platform to drum the thoughts out with my feet. She wouldn't leave me here, would she? I check my phone for messages. The small of my back is sticky from effort, so I stop to watch a buzzard as it loops the distant field and warn it away with my finger when it changes direction towards me.

Maybe Mae is worried that people will think I'm peculiar. She needn't worry. I'm not going to admit to anyone all the weird things that happen around me. I'm not going to tell anyone that some people have called me a…

'Wilde!' Mae's silver sequinned flip-flops make it hard for her to run. She flump-trip-flumps towards me, stubs her toe and swears. 'I'm late. I'm so sorry.'

'It doesn't matter, Mae.' It matters.

'The car. It's the heat. She's temperamental. It's so good to see you. My goodness, you've grown.'

She grabs me in a hopping hug which lasts too long. Releases me. Hugs me again. Half releases me so that we are standing too close together. Awkward. We carry the awkwardness with us as we walk to the car.

'Why are you wearing all black? You must be boiling.'

'I like black, that's all.'

'Where is Mrs Lee?'

'I told her to go.' A lie. Mrs Lee was snoring like a cow when I scarpered. I left her a note so she wouldn't worry. I had to haul myself through a window and shin down a tree. It's not easy to break out of a boarding school, though I'm getting better at it. Some of my plait still hangs on a branch as a final goodbye. When you have to leave, do it quickly. Not escorted out under a shame cloud and definitely not accompanied by a disapproving adult on a three-hour train trip filled with tea and tuts.

'She needed to go because you were late – she had to get back to teach Latin. Et cetera.' My lie fizzes and stings. Lies always hurt.

I'm not good at school. I don't fit in. Things always go wrong and I have to cause trouble and leave.

'You have a twig in your hair. Shall we go home?'

Home.

Mae clambers in through the passenger side and scoots across to the driver's, getting one of the rips in her jean-shorts caught on the gearstick, so she has to tear them a bit more to free herself. 'I'm glad,' she says, as I get in. 'I could do with a bit more ventilation.'

She is a silver-lining finder, that's for sure.

Flapping at her face with one hand, she unwinds her window with the other. 'Come on, Vera. You can do this, old girl,' she tells the car, patting the steering wheel. 'This heat is intolerable. I feel like a tomato.'

I could tell her that she doesn't look like one, but I've lied enough already.

'Vera is a little terror to get going but once she's started, she's a dream.'

The car hacks into life. Chill-out music plays over the engine, pan pipes and chimes. As we get going, the wind blasts in through the windows like a hairdryer stuck fast on hot.

'I'm so glad you are here. I mean, I'm not, obviously, because you should have done well at that last school. It took a long time for your dad to find someone who'd take you. But I am as well. You know?'

Mae looks different from when she used to visit during the holidays. Older. I think of the thing she told me about my mum that I keep hidden way, deep down inside. I swallow it deeper. My stomach churns. I should have eaten something. Too nervous. I take in a long burning breath, unstick my legs from the seats, blow out slowly.

Long gardens, garages, a trampoline on its side, an abandoned trike and a kid using a dustbin lid as a shield against the sun. According to legend, Witch Point is cursed. Everyone tries to leave and if they escape, they hardly ever come back. This is where my mum and dad grew up. This is where I lived till I was two. I don't want to stay in a place where they talk about witches. I don't want to think about curses. I stare out of the window, concentrate on what's outside, to stop the pain inside.

We pass a cemetery which is slowly sliding down the hill. Most of the shops and cafés on the high street are witch-themed or boarded up. I count the smells: melting plastic; suffocating exhaust fumes: all the roasting aromas of Vera.

'Eww. What's that doing there?'

A gallows stands, dark and macabre, in the town square.

'Just an attraction to bring tourists in.'

'I would think it would send them straight back out.'

The noose is missing and only part of a threadbare rope remains. Someone has hung something from it. When we get close enough, I'm relieved to see it's a toy. *Sick thing to do, all the same.*

'It's the curse,' Mae mutters under her breath.

'I don't believe in curses,' I insist.

'Tell that to the clockmakers.'

I don't know what that's supposed to mean so I don't say anything.

'Whenever there's a funeral in that church, the clock strikes thirteen times.'

'It's just a broken clock. Nothing to do with a curse.'

'Margaret Morris was crossing here and she got hit on the head by a fish. It swam straight out of the sky.'

'A freak event. They happen everywhere.'

'In the same spot, Jonathan Jones got hit by lightning; then exactly a year later his son got hit by lightning.'

'They should avoid that spot then.'

'They put it down to coincidence and a year later…'

'Don't tell me, his wife got hit by lightning.'

'No, his dog.'

'Oh, that's awful.'

'It survived, but it went from a red setter to white.'

I hate it when bad things happen to animals.

'And, as you know, the legend says that in the end the town will be plagued by a terrifying heat and everyone will die. I don't know if you've noticed Wilde but it's pretty hot at the moment.'

The curse sounds more convincing than I'd expected, but I'm not going to admit it.

Vera starts up the lane, then stops. The engine rattles and groans like my stomach.

'I hope you like the house.' Mae struggles out and retrieves my case from the back seat. I take it from her. The clasp is fragile and I don't want it to pop and scatter my belongings all over the lane. There isn't much in the case. I've just brought the important things: a seagull's skull, the *Complete Works of Shakespeare*, a photo of my mum and me when I was a baby, two sticks of rock, a folder of my favourite future travel destinations, basic clothes and a broken raven brooch I never leave behind.

We pant up the last bit of the hill and turn the

corner. The house scrutinizes me. I feel smaller than a toddler under its inspection.

'It's OK. Witch Point House has been waiting for you.'

Gulp.

Craning my neck, I take it all in. It's imposing. It has three chimneys and a weathervane in the shape of a stretching cat. The windows are all slanted, as if the house is leaning, and there are lanterns and bells hanging from every ledge.

'It's different.' I'm doing my best.

'Different is good.' Mae strides ahead and I trot the path behind her, holding my suitcase together.

'Why are the windows wonky?'

'They are witch windows. Slanted to stop a witch from flying in. Hilarious, really.'

'Stupid.' I laugh. I'm glad we agree it's ridiculous.

'As if a witch can't fly sideways.'

The arched-back weathervane cat moves without a breath of wind, then springs off, and I realise it is Mrs Danvers, Mae's cat. The weathervane she has been sleeping in front of is a girl riding a bear.

'She's being a bit of a sourpuss, because she likes to have all the attention. She'll calm down in a bit.' Mae flip-flap-flops up the steps and adjusts a telescope on the porch. I hang back.

Home.

The witch windows throw out diagonal sky sapphires. In the Victorian conservatory, healing plants wilt. Heady scents of lavender and jasmine, saffron and rambling rose swirl out. Colourful homemade potions sparkle like rock pools. Mae makes cosmetics and remedies with natural ingredients. She cured me of whooping cough when I was a baby and mended Dad's broken leg when he fell off his bike. Or so the story goes.

Further across the garden I can see a treehouse. Now that is something to be excited about.

'Your room is right at the top.' Mae hangs over the balustrade and points to a slanted window at the very tip of the house. 'You can see the sea in the distance from there.'

'Perfect.' I am already planning my nights in the treehouse.

Mae pushes open the door. 'Welcome, Wilde. We've been expecting you.'

Shadows skitter and still. Pentacle tiles, blue against silver, nestle under my feet. A breeze tickles the back of my neck.

I turn and something flies up the stairs.

'I've told the animals to give you a chance to settle in before they welcome you. They can be a bit overwhelming *en masse*.'

'I'd like to meet them all now.' The only animals I can see are the birds painted on the walls. 'Why haven't I been here since I was a baby?'

'That, Wilde, is complicated.'

Mae's phone makes a noise like a werewolf howling at the moon and she goes outside to answer it.

The hall is gloomy cool with the blue stained-glass panels filtering the light. Almost like swimming. Drowning.

I watch the shadows shuffle. Something moves in the mirror, in the corner of my eye. I feel the shiver of strange all over me. I plunge down into the azure depths, searching for a slippery-fish memory I can't quite catch. Mae brings me back to the surface.

'That was Mrs Lee informing me of how you left. What a stupid and dangerous thing to do, Wilde.' Mae puts her phone on the hallstand and I prepare myself for an argument. Instead she turns around and extends her hand for my phone. 'At least you aren't grounded.'

I give it over and sulk.

'Don't worry. Your dad has given me the times he'll call, so you'll be able to speak to him.'

As if that's the only thing people use their phones for.

Mae takes my suitcase and I snatch it back.

'The clasp is a bit faulty. It's an old one. I just want to make sure nothing falls out.' I don't like people having my things, in case I need to run. 'I'll take it up.'

'Just keep on going till you can't go any further. It has a picture of a llama on the door so you can't miss it.'

'Why a llama?'

'Why not?'

I start the Everest stairs.

'I'll put the kettle on. No, wait. You're young. I'll make us lemonade. I've never done it before, but it can't be that difficult.' Mae's flip-flops slap away then stop. 'Wilde?'

I halt mid-flight.

'I'm not very good at this but I'm going to give it my very best shot.'

I nod to show I'm going to do the same.

At the top of the stairs there is a photo of Mae acting. She is wearing a tiara and impossibly high heels. Along the threadbare carpet, up another flight, followed by another – smaller for servants who didn't get as much to eat, so didn't need fat stairs.

The door creaks open. Laid out on a chair is a school uniform in green and gold. Bleurgh. Mae and Dad want me to go to Witch Point Primary, even though the term is almost over, so I can make some friends before the summer holidays. It's the most ridiculous idea anyone ever had. I can't really argue because Dad is already livid with me. I meant it when I promised him I'd be on my best behaviour while he was away working. He's researching cures for diabetes, so other people won't die of it like Mum did. It's important. Dad is the best dad and I've let him down. I should have stuck it out, but the bullies were just too much. Again. Is it my fault? If I could be normal, would they stop picking on me?

I put my suitcase near the door, where I can grab it quickly if necessary, and sit on the bed. The springs squeak, so I bounce a bit for fun and make a horrendous noise.

Home.

A single word has so much power.

I practise being Normal. Cross my legs and tilt my head as if I'm listening to someone. Fold my arms and pretend to be having a scintillating conversation. Stand up and walk about at different speeds. I'm going to have to practise lots.

Peering through the slanted window, I long for that shiver of sea on the horizon.

'Lemonade.'

Mae comes in and puts the tumbler down on an old worn desk. 'It's like drinking washing-up liquid so I brought you a jug of water to swill the taste away.'

'Thank you.'

'You won't say that once you've tasted it. It's so good to have you here. Properly. I'm really thrilled, and we are going to have so much fun.' She runs her hand along the empty bookshelf and loads her fingerprints with dust. 'It's going to be fine. Fun,' she repeats. 'And there's plenty of room for your things.'

Talking of fun: 'How do I use your wi-fi without my phone?'

'I'm afraid, Wilde, that I find having wi-fi on all

14

the time in my house completely unmanageable. The waves in the air give me a headache. Also, I have no willpower when it comes to online shopping, so, for the most part, I manage without.'

I search for an answer and come up with nothing. Taking a sip of lemonade to be polite, I have to suck my cheeks to hold the disgust in.

'I'll introduce you to the animals tomorrow.' Mae is notorious for letting any waif and stray into her house. 'Of course, you know Mrs Danvers, because I brought her on holiday with me.'

'Yes, she's adorable.' The lie ricochets, whizzes past my ear, then bounces off the wall to clip the back of my head.

'Isn't she?' Mae pats a space for me to sit, smoothing the choppy waves of duvet. 'Let's meditate.'

Let's not, I think, but I sit and let her close her eyes. I want to show I'm grateful to her. The Witch Point uniform sits on the chair like it already has a person inside it. I wish it would walk away. The jitter of first day nerves jolts through me and I bite one of my nails too low. I've been to lots of schools. Why am I still so scared?

Outside the window, the day burns itself out. A fox slips through the bushes at the end of the garden, bushy tail quivering. The day pinks into lavender, stars button the sky, a chitter rises from the brittle parched grasses. The sea lines the edge of the distance and pulls at me. Soon everything is shadows and I am full of ache.

Mae gets up and flicks on the light. 'Now. Isn't that better?'

'Yes, much.' This time, the lie gnaws the inside of my cheek, as vicious as Mae's lemonade.

'Will you be OK up here?'

I nod.

She blows a kiss and leaves the door ajar.

Wrestling my daps off, I wriggle my swollen toes. I could try to make the most of it here. It's not long till the holidays and surely Mae won't mind if I don't go to school? I can tell her I'm too traumatised, or simply be honest. Some people don't make friends easily because they are too shy. Some people are weird and mess everything up. Some people have to cause trouble and leave even if they aren't troublemakers at all and doing it terrifies them.

The ceiling of my room is v-shaped, so I duck

into the corners to check for spiders. I feel better when I find some. I like to watch them knit their webs and dangle on the draughts. Not that there is any draught. The skylight is open to the stars. Not a breath of air for anyone in Witch Point.

Emptying my possessions from my case I place them on the shelf. One of the raven's legs is broken and its silver is so tarnished it looks more like gold. When I have enough money, I'm going to get its leg soldered. For now, I put it back in its box to sleep.

The sticks of rock ooze inside the cellophane, but they remind me of the yellow flat where I live with Dad, so I open one and bite off the end to combat the taste of bitter lemons.

My Shakespeare book is heavy and takes up lots of space in my case, which is why I can never pack many clothes when I run. I lift it up and brush the travel fluff from the cover. I take the seagull skull out and delicately kiss it. I flick through my travel plans to make sure they are undamaged. One day I'm going to set off around the world and never come back. The photo of my mum goes next to the bed. She looks happy there caught in a rectangle of waterfall and river.

Claiming the room with my things makes it feel better. Music swans its way up the stairs. I've heard it before. It's called 'Fly Me to the Moon' and the singer is a crooner called Frank somebody or other. I lie back on the bed and let the song filter through my body. I wish I had my phone so I could listen to something good instead. I concentrate on choosing where I'm going to live when I have my own life. Venezuela, near Angel Falls? Canada, somewhere with bears? Norway, so I can see the Northern Lights? For now, I'm here, like it or not.

Another chapter starts. Will it be a good one?

The question keeps me from falling asleep. Until it doesn't.

2

School. The first day. Is there anything more awful in the whole wide world? Even though I've had plenty of practice at starting new schools, I never get used to it. If anything, it gets worse.

My legs wobble as I walk across the yard, concentrating on not tripping over.

Everyone else has friends already. They all walk about in pairs, threes, or gangs, hollering out to each other and guffawing with laughter. A girl lassoes her bag over her head with jubilant whoops, until the strap snaps. It thwacks a boy in the chest. A shove flares into a fight and spectators break the four-minute mile to get a ringside view. Two teachers appear from nowhere, trying to retain an air of authority as they leg it into the fray.

I follow the lines from *Macbeth* painted on the tarmac, which point the way to the reception.

When shall we three meet again,

In thunder, lightning, or in rain?

My mum was in lots of Shakespeare plays with Mae. That's how she met my dad. It's a long story, which comes out at special occasions.

When the hurlyburly's done,
When the battle's lost and won
That will be ere the set of sun.

All the other schools I've been to have hands pointing the way, or yellow footprints. I'm sure they've chosen these words instead because Witch Point has a history of witchcraft and I really wish they hadn't, but the Shakespeare is a good sign all the same.

Where the place?
Upon the heath.

I find reception and wait for someone to notice me while trying my best to disappear. A man with huge teeth slides back the thumb-printed glass and grins out at me. His teeth are coffee-coloured and he has breath to match.

'There to meet with Macbeth!' He waits for me to join in. I know the line but I just squirm.

'Oh, don't you know the great play? We are very big on drama at this school. *Macbeth* is a play by Shakespeare. We have lots of copies in the library.'

I smile. Part of me wants to tell him that at one of my schools I made a replica of the Globe Theatre using matchsticks and slid it across the frozen Thames (made from kitchen foil) to see how they had managed it, but I figure most girls my age wouldn't have done that kind of thing, and I'm on a mission to blend in.

'New, are we?'

I nod.

'Excellent. Then you'll be…' He flicks through a green and gold folder with the school's Witch Point emblem on it. A witch, a raven and a waterfall. It's unusual.

'Wilde Jenkins. Yes, here we are. Good name. Wait! What am I saying? Great name! This way!'

He buzzes the door.

'You probably already know this info but I'm going to give you the lowdown anyway.'

He leads me through a labyrinth of corridors. 'The school has been here since the year 1783 and before it became a school it was a workhouse.'

I guess most pupils wouldn't find this stuff interesting. I do, but I don't respond so that I can seem normal.

'You'll notice most of the classrooms are empty.

Lots of the children are out on trips. Big Pit. It's a mine that was closed down. They make you turn off your helmet lights. Truly terrifying. Or the Brecon Beacons: survival skills, eating beetles and the like, I should think. Horrid. Some of them have gone on a coastal writers' residency in North Wales. I'd like to do that. I have a novel I've been working on for a while, but luckily for you we have reached your class, so I won't bore you with the details.'

I'd rather listen to every detail of his novel than face my new class.

'Here we are – Year Six.'

Peering nervously through the gridded glass, I can see a mixture of faces like a maths problem laid out on a graph. The equals, equals scared.

'Welcome to your new tribe.'

I'm led into a room of stares. A fly headbutts the window, trying to get out. I know just how it feels.

'Mr Ricketts. New victim here for you.'

No one laughs except Mr Ricketts and the receptionist, whose smile has taken on Big Bad Wolf proportions. Mr Ricketts wears a salmon jumper and has a quiff like a fish fin. His tan shoes have metal taps to save his heels that click-tackety-click as he walks towards me. I worry he might start tap-dancing.

'Come in. Don't be shy.'

Shy people hate it when you call them out on it. It makes shyness sound like a disease.

I hope he doesn't try to make me introduce myself to everyone with Three Interesting Facts:

I'm very Normal.

I have no other interesting facts.

I refer you to point two.

I shuffle from foot to foot and try really hard to be The Same.

Mr Ricketts raps his heels like he's finished his routine. 'Class. Can I have your attention, please?'

He needn't have asked. Everyone is giving me every bit of their attention. Even the fly has stopped buzzing and is pointing my way.

'This is…'

'Wilde,' I blurt out, then feel shame climb up my face. A snigger from a yellow-haired girl with the highest possible ponytail. She follows it with mocking, sly eyes to her friends. I force my head up. I've done this loads of times now. I can handle this.

'Wilde is new to us today, so I need you to be

nice to her, please. You'll all recognise how nerve-wracking it is to be going to a new school, but when you go up to Witch Point High at least you'll know each other. Wilde doesn't know anyone yet. She isn't from here.'

'You can tell.' That girl again, twirling her hair round her fingers innocently and looking me up and down. 'What, Sir? It's just an observation.'

Even in a uniform I still don't match.

'Jemima, please.'

She mutters, 'So unfair.'

'Jemima. That's a warning. I don't want to have to tell you again.' Mr Ricketts glares at her.

I feel like an ant, being burned under a sun-filled magnifying glass by loathsome children.

'We have been using a chalkboard because we have been studying the Victorians, Wilde. Do you know much about the Victorian era?'

I shake my head. I try to avoid making eye contact with Jemima, but eventually I have to look. She meets me with a wasp-sting stare.

Excellent start. One minute in the classroom = one enemy already. I may as well have admitted that I know lots about the Victorians and given her ammunition. *Actually, I know lots about different historical eras, Jemima, because I have been to lots of schools and learned lots of different things. Yes, I am an interesting specimen. Thank you for noticing.*

'There's no need for us to find you a seat just yet, Wilde, because you have arrived on a very exciting day.'

The class seem anything but excited. A couple of them groan.

'We have the extraordinarily thrilling opportunity of working on a Page to Stage project with an – and I use her own words here – "outstanding actress" to help us. We don't have long till the end of term so let's make this project count please, Year Six.'

More groans.

A Climate Emergency poster unpeels itself from the wall and slithers to the floor in protest. A girl runs to put it back, her curls bouncing like bubbles exploding from a champagne bottle. She gives me the biggest smile, and I smile fully back because she's friendly and she obviously thinks that halting global warming is important, then stare at my feet again. New shoes. Must scuff them urgently.

'So, we are all off to the hall. Single file, please.

Keep the noise down. Wilde, you can come with me, so we can get to know each other a bit.'

Chalk my outline. I. Want. To. Die. Right. Now.

A boy who looks like a tortoise, his head is so far down inside his collar, jumps out of his seat. 'Sir, I forgot. I need to have my behaviour slip signed for yesterday.'

'Oh yes, Lewis. Of course. Two seconds, Wilde, if you...'

'It's alright, Sir. She can come with us.' Jemima pushes forward, closely followed by her sidekicks. She links her arm through mine and yanks me to the door before Mr Ricketts can stop her.

'Best behaviour. I'm warning you,' he yells after us. As soon as we are through the door, the others break loose.

'I'm Jemima. Mimes to my friends. So, you can call me Jemima.' She flicks her ponytail from side to side as she walks. A couple of times it slaps me in the face. 'This is Holly and Ivy. They are twins. *Obviously.*'

She says this as if I lack the intelligence to work it out for myself. I try to smile, but my lips stick to my teeth. I nod vigorously instead.

'Your name is Wilde, right?' She screws her face up in disdain. 'Weird name, right?'

My head feels dizzy from all the nodding.

'Is it a nickname?'

I shake my head.

'So, it's short for something?'

Shake.

'So, your name is Wilde and that's your REAL name?' Jemima is horrified and thrilled at the same time. 'I mean, just to clarify, your parents actually called you *Wilde*?'

Holly and Ivy giggle.

'Don't be nasty, girls.' Jemima smiles at them overly brightly and they stop. 'So, what's your story, Wilde?'

I don't want to tell her my story. I have to say something. 'Oh, you know. Nothing.'

'As I suspected.' She looks me up and down critically. 'Where did you get your uniform from? Is it secondhand?' She acts as if she might pass out on the floor, she is so offended by it.

'I'm taking a stand against disposable fashion to try to save the planet.'

'I see.'

Holly and Ivy snicker as she leads them into the

hall. 'Come on, girls. Time for me to get my starring role.'

They strut off ahead, their ponytails swishing in unison.

I loosen the horrible Witch Point tie and twist my skirt around the right way. My shirt is too small, and the skirt is too gross. I'm trying to be grateful to Mae for sorting it out at such short notice, but some unrepeatable words run through my head.

The walls are covered in dark pictures which watch me skulking through the corridors: standing stones and skies filled with corvids; a man in a fox skin holding a crescent-moon sickle and a tall-hatted witch-hunter general; a witch being tried by a judge; seven women dancing in a circle, with a horrible hag-like figure spying on them. I've known the legend of 'The Witch Called Winter' since I was little. I bet everyone in the world knows it. It feels closer here, where her story started.

I want to go home. To Dad's. With my real own room and my view out over the changing sea. Perhaps I should cause trouble today and get kicked out super swiftly so I can home-school myself instead of having to do time here. I don't need friends. I don't need anyone. I am made of ice. I can teach myself astronomy by looking at the stars and Mae can teach me herbalism before I go. I won't make an effort to make any friends here, because I definitely, certainly, won't be staying.

A whirlwind of energy rushes up to me. It's the girl with the popped cork hair.

'Don't worry about The Sleeks. They are like that with literally everyone. I'm Dorcas. Pleased to meet you. Your name is NOTHING compared to mine when it comes to bullying. BELIEVE. Can you speak Spanish? I'm learning. My birth dad is Nigerian, so he speaks Igbo, and my step-dad, he's my proper dad really, is Indian and speaks Hindi, and my mum has travelled all over and speaks all sorts of languages. I'm also learning guitar, slowly. Too slowly, really, I'm thinking of giving it up for the flute. Sorry, information overload. I talk too much. *Hola.*'

She puts her hand out for me to shake it. I want to but feel self-conscious.

'Don't worry. You don't have to shake hands. Lots of diseases are carried through hand contact, did you know that? You could get bubonic plague from an escalator handrail.'

My ice cracks a bit, because this is exactly the kind of fact I like. Could Dorcas be a kindred spirit? I've been looking for one for so long.

We shuffle to the end of the line, far away from The Sleeks, and sit on the floor. I hate sitting on the floor. It always ends up with someone having a squashed pea on their clothes, no matter which school you go to.

'This should be fun. It gets us out of class anyway.'

Dorcas turns to talk to the boy on the other side of her, and I try not to feel conspicuous. The thick smell of gravy slides through the kitchen slats. Dust motes flitter in the sunlight. The world glitters outside.

Mr Ricketts arrives looking bothered.

'Sir, are you alright? You look really hot.'

'I'm fine, thank you, Jemima.'

'Can I give you some advice, Sir?'

He doesn't answer. I don't blame him.

'A pink jumper doesn't complement your complexion, Sir.'

'What insightful advice, Jemima. I'll be sure to put it into practice in my fashion-conscious life.'

Good for him. He asks for silence while he

takes another register, even though we've only walked a couple of hundred yards.

'Hand it over, please.' He puts his hand out to Jemima and she gets up and walks to him stroppily. 'I don't know how many times I have to say it, Year Six. Phones are not allowed in school.'

At least I already fit with that.

'But it's my personal property, Sir.'

'And, as I've told you a million times, you'll get it back at the end of the day.'

'That's tantamount to stealing, Sir.' She gives it to him and strops back to her place grumbling and making as much fuss as she can.

'Settle down, please. Jemima Morgan, I said settle down.'

'Sorry, Sir. It's just it's practically child abuse to expect us to sit on the floor.'

'Enough.'

'I'm getting a letter from home.'

'I said enough.'

'And a lawyer.'

'Second warning of the day. I think that's a record even for you.'

He scratches his neck and I can see he has

psoriasis between his fingers. I bet it is caused by
Jemima.

'Now, Year Six, we are very lucky to have this
brilliant opportunity, so I expect you to show
respect for our esteemed guest and for each other.
We'd like to extend a very warm Witch Point
welcome to Gwyneth Fox-Rutherford.'

He starts the class off clapping, but most of
them don't need an excuse to make a noise. I join
in and whoop a couple of times. It feels really
good.

Once the applause has reached raucous, a
woman so short and round she looks like an egg
on legs, bursts into the room and bounces to
centre stage with her arms open wide, as if she is
going to ask us all to come in for a group hug.

'Thank you. Thank you. *Diolch*, which means
thank you in Welsh.' She picks up her orange
velvet skirt and curtsies.

The class stop clapping abruptly because this is
basic Welsh, not worth the meal she is making of
it. I feel bad for her, so clap again, then sit on my
hands.

'Thank you, Mr Ricketts. I am   honoured
to be here.   DEEPLY

32

Did you see that children? How I reflected my feelings with the pitch of my voice. Oh, I'm sorry, Mr Ricketts, I'm educating them already. I simply can't help myself. It's in the blood, isn't it? Teaching. Such a noble cause.'

Mr Ricketts beams at her. He gives the class his best warning-without-words and leaves with Lewis in tow because, now he's had his behaviour card signed, he is playing up and needs to be taken to Time Out.

'Rapt audience. Well, you might be! For we are here to create art. Real art.'

'Are we drawing, Miss?'

'No, we are going to become thespians. Actors. Devisors. Playwrights and performers.' She rolls her Rs and hits every consonant crisply. 'Ah, I remember giving my King Lear at Sadler's Wells. It was the first time a woman had played the role on that stage, I believe. It is one of many characters to which I have given birth…'

She begins to reel through a huge list of other parts. I'm disappointed she is more interested in sounding successful than in the characters she was playing. I think about the Globe Theatre in London. I went there once. There is no roof in the middle. It's round and open to the skies, the clouds and the birds. The owl on the station platform. The jackdaw and the crow joining it. The weirdness I can't lose.

'Are you alright, dear?'

Gwyneth Fox-Rutherford is waving her hand in front of my face. I must have been daydreaming. Everyone is staring at me. Jemima is loving every second of it.

'I'm fine.'

'I'll open a window. The air will revive you. And then we will begin our retelling of the wonderful legend, The Witch Called Winter.'

No.

Groans from the class and a discontented mumble. Gwyneth bounds over to the windows, oblivious to the fact the class don't like her choice any more than I do. She's too short to reach the window latches so some of the children have to help her. Jemima is staring at me like she knows how weird I am. There is a cold sheen of sweat on my skin. I manage a weak smile. Everything tastes of Mae's lemonade. Bitter and sharp and medicinal.

Gwyneth sits cross-legged on the edge of the

stage again. 'Focus in, folks. Let us begin with our terrible tale of witchery.'

'Miss, can't we do *Spiderman* or something?'

'Seriously, we've been doing Winter in assembly since we were born.'

'What about *Titanic*, Miss?'

'The suffragettes. Were they terrorists or freedom fighters?'

'Mary Anning and her fossils.'

'Rosa Parks.'

'Martin Luther King. I have a dream.'

These all get whoops from the class. I'm impressed too and am going to add about Amelia Earhart being the first woman to fly the Atlantic and landing in south Wales, but Gwyneth holds her hands up patronisingly. She shifts position and looks doleful.

'Such a shame. All this calling out is making me feel very uncomfortable on the inside.'

She shifts position again. She is clearly uncomfortable on the outside too.

'I can't share with you young people unless you are willing to listen. This makes me feel very sad.'

'Yeah. Listen, everyone.' Jemima has a way of

stopping people talking. I don't know why everyone listens to her. They just do.

'Thank you, Jemima.'

'You are very welcome, Gwyneth.'

Jemima smugs in my direction.

I imagine saying to her, *No, I'm not weird. I'm perfectly Normal, thank you. That thing where I zoned out? I just don't feel very well. It's probably a stomach bug. You know what schools are like for incubating germs.*

A crow flies into the hall through the open window and lands in my lap. Chaos erupts.

After ten minutes of arms and wings, Gwyneth Fox-Rutherford still stands centre stage, cowering with her hands up to her face.

'Miss, it's gone, Miss.'

She unpeels her fingers and shudders, then straightens up and looks very proud of herself.

'Did you see how I played the part of a person who is afraid of birds? Did you? Convincing, wasn't it?' She beams at us. 'I think it deserves a small mark of appreciation.'

Starting the clapping off herself, she gets a smattering this time and lots of doubtful faces.

'Now, focus in, guys. Good news! A proclamation! Because it is so ridiculously hot today, we have Mr Ricketts' permission to work in the yard.'

A mixture of cheers and the groans which seem to be Year Six's speciality. Everyone starts calling out complaints about bee stings, anaphylactic shock, sunglasses, lack of water, skin cancer, as we all stand up and check our clothes for peas. Gwyneth is ready with suntan lotion and instructs everyone to slather it all over themselves. Some end up looking like ghosts.

'Let us enjoy the open air and give our drama to the sun.'

The class traipses out, Gwyneth leading the way. I lag behind and try to stop myself shaking. Why did the crow have to land right in my lap? Why not someone else's?

I'm so tired of causing trouble everywhere I go. I want to be happy. Can I get rid of the weird here or will it be with me for life?

3

Raised voices skitter upstairs. I ask Mrs Danvers, 'Seriously, who has the energy in this heat?'

Mrs Danvers answers me by jumping on to the bed, where she curls up like a comma, then stretches into an exclamation mark, her tail tapping the dot. We are beginning to tolerate each other.

'I suppose I'd better go down and find out what's going on.' I close the folder on pictures of Peru and put it back on the shelf. I spoke to Dad earlier. He's glad that I'm doing a Page to Stage project at school because he thinks it will make me happy. I suppose because theatre made my mum happy. I didn't tell him it's about witches.

I change out of my uniform, smelling the armpits of my shirt to see if it will last another day, nearly vomiting, and throwing it in a ball on the floor. I put on my favourite black T-shirt and a pair of black shorts and check myself in the mirror. Something shifts at the corner of the silver glass. I spin around.

Nothing. The heat up here is making me hallucinate. I need to cool down.

Some old-person track is turned on in the kitchen. Creeping downstairs, I startle a duck having a nap in the hall. Animals turn up in every nook and cranny here. I share the bathroom with a field mouse and when I went to brush my hair this morning there was a frog sitting on the bristles.

Peering into the drawing room I see a big dog loping about with his tail wagging, his ears so long they practically scrape the floor. I put my knuckles to his nose so he can smell me. He leans in to let me give him a good scratch behind his ears. The name on his collar reads 'Denzel'.

'Hello, Denzel.'

He licks my hand hello then lopes off to lie under the piano. I hear loud voices again and find Mae teetering on a chair in the kitchen, trying to reach some daisy-shaped flowers on a high shelf. She must have been shouting at herself. There are flowers everywhere. It smells like a wedding. She takes a deep gulp of some blue, bubbly concoction.

'How many of those have you had?'

'Too many and also not enough. Would you like one?'

'I'm fairly sure it's against the law for me to drink.'

'Oh, for goodness sake. Who cares about laws?'

'Normal people.'

'Who wants to be normal? It's more than a little dull.'

Dull sounds good to me. Epic, in fact.

She's in a mood because they've employed Gwyneth Fox-Rutherford to do the drama project. Mae has run some of their other drama productions and when I told her about this new one, she was furious. That's why I've been hiding out in my room.

Mae gets down from the chair and sprays her face with the stuff she's been using for the flowers. 'Ah, essence of gardenia. Do you think it's wrong to spray a flower with another flower?'

'Why don't you ask them?' I smile sweetly.

'Ask the flowers. Of course. Why didn't I think of that?'

I open the door of the fridge and try to fit myself in it.

Mae starts to sway, her voice warbling strange, strangled chicken sounds. An actual chicken walks in and cocks its head, as if assessing whether Mae is in pain or not. Mrs Danvers runs out through the cat flap. Mae's skirt hem is torn at the back and opens like a mouth as she moves. She belches, then sits heavily opposite me, as if she is going to start a deep and meaningful lecture. I am saved by the arrival of Mae's partner, Jules. She has stayed at ours before and we get on like a house on fire.

'Guess what? Wilde's school is doing a drama production and they've only gone and got another practitioner in to run it!' Mae scowls. 'They shouldn't have people coming in. We could have done it here. In the garden. That would have been perfect, wouldn't it, Wilde?'

I give Jules a pleading look and she gets it immediately.

'Wilde, could you please go and check on the animals? Take some water.' Jules winks and I rush out.

Most of the animals are hiding in any available

shade outside. The duck splashes in a washing-up bowl of water. A donkey is lying down under a cherry blossom tree, which is unusual. Not that there's a donkey in the garden, which seems to be quite ordinary here, but the fact it is lying down. The chicken wanders about, *buk-buking* into a hole under the hedge. Mrs Danvers, seeing me, slinks off in a different direction. I top up the water bowls, pat the donkey's nose and jump at the size of her teeth.

The treehouse will be the best place for shade, I'm certain. It's majestic and inviting, way above me in the ancient oak tree. I want to sleep out here, but I have to wait till I've got Mae on side. She's worked hard to make the house welcoming for me.

The first rung of the ladder is easy, but I get sweaty by the second. My clothes stick to my skin and my lungs threaten to pop by the time I get to the top. Standing on the platform, which runs around the outside, I whistle at the view through dry lips. It is gorgeous. Forgotten and a bit weather-beaten, but perfect.

Inside, hazy green light shuffles delicate patterns across the floor. I'm going to ask Mae if I can bring the telescope up from the porch and stargaze from here. I bet I'll be able to see Jupiter and the Milky Way.

The treehouse hasn't been used for a while. There's a pile of decaying twigs in the corner where something has made a nest and then abandoned it. Everything needs a bit of tender loving care, but I make a solemn promise that I am going to bring it back to life and treasure it for as long as I'm here.

Poking my head out of one window, I can see an enchanting dark green forest crawling up the hills behind Witch Point. Poking my head out of the other window, I find Mrs Danvers staring back crossly.

'Sorry, Mrs D.'

I leave her in peace and go out onto the platform again, imagining the garden as the theatre space it used to be.

Over the hedge, a head of familiar effervescent curls is passing. It's now or never. I'm so sick of being lonely.

'Hello,' I call, half hoping that Dorcas won't hear me.

She looks up and the surprise on her face

makes me laugh. I guess this place is camouflaged from the outside by the leaves.

I give her a big wave.

'Wilde! You have a treehouse! That is the most amazing thing in the world. Can I come up? I've always wanted a treehouse and we could never have one in our garden because it's too small and we only have a lemon tree that comes up to my waist. I mean it will grow, but at the moment a treehouse would squash it splat flat and I guess then it would be a shed, not a treehouse.'

Even Dorcas has to stop for breath.

I'm shy. I'm always shy. It comes from being hurt too many times.

It's cool in here. I have shade. I should share the shade.

'Come up.'

I go back in without waiting for an answer.

I wish I'd had time to tidy the treehouse so that Dorcas could be wowed by it. She's taking a long time. Perhaps she's realised I'm not worth it and gone away. I hold my breath and listen for her. I hear the tree sighing. An ice-cream van in the distance. Dorcas on the rungs.

'This isn't easy.'

I dash out on to the platform. Dorcas is climbing the ladder with a tray on her head.

'I mean, I know that in some areas of the world people carry things like this all the time, but I've not had any practice.'

The tray tips and the jug slides precariously close to the edge. I lie flat on my tummy and reach down, trying to grab it from her when she gets close enough. We both end up in fits of laughter. Eventually I've got it, and then she is up.

'Your aunt gave it to me. The ice cubes are melting already. She offered to help me up with it, but I said I was fine. You live and learn.'

'Yes. You do.'

I remember all my past failed friendships. All the people who saw my weird. I look at Dorcas and her brilliant smile. I'm going to let myself try.

'Come into the treehouse.'

She lets me walk in first. I put the tray down on a stump in the corner.

'Wow. This place is amazing.'

'I've only just come up here myself. I haven't had time to tidy it. I'm sorry it's a bit of a mess.' I don't know why I'm apologising. I just want Dorcas to like it. To like me.

'What's untidy about it? It's awesome. Do you sleep up here? I would definitely sleep in here if I could. Can we? I mean, shall we? One day? Night, I mean? Sleep up here?'

I laugh. Her energy is infectious.

'Yes. OK.' My heart lifts, like a swift soaring on thermals, but I manage to act nonchalant all the same. 'Shall we drink this before the ice cubes melt?'

I pour, grateful the drink is water and not homemade lemonade. Dorcas gulps hers down in one and then lies back on the wooden boards. I sit and sip mine, listening to the fragments of ice tinkling the glass. The sun is slowly giving up work for the day, the shafts low and peach. Dorcas runs her hand through one of them, blocking the light and then setting it free again, as if she can make light appear by magic. I steer clear of that word even in my brain.

'Did you know that most dust is made up of human skin?'

She sits up abruptly. I nod.

'Why are you called Wilde? I mean, it's a cool name and everything, but it's unusual, right?'

I nod again. I don't talk about my mum much. I take a deep breath of dusk and go for it.

'My mum went to a famous cemetery in Paris. It's called *Père Lachaise*. It's got lots of famous people in it. Singers and composers and writers. Loads of people go there to see the mausoleums, tombs like houses with stained-glass windows. Dad said it's very moving. Anyway, they were there on a beautiful autumn day and my mum was really into Shakespeare.'

I wait for scorn or a dig of some kind, but Dorcas just looks interested, so I carry on.

'She was kicking up leaves and trying names out. Dad said she was about eight months pregnant and looked like a cavorting angel with a very big belly.'

Dorcas laughs then leans in encouragingly. I think she can sense this is a big deal to me.

'She wanted to call me something Shakespearean. Desdemona or Ophelia. But she told my dad she was waiting for me to kick so that she knew I agreed. She had to stop and have a rest and she sat on a bench by Oscar Wilde's grave. Apparently, it's big and like a sphinx. And people are so moved by his life story and the things that he wrote that they leave notes and presents and candles all over it. So many that they have to clear it every day to make room for new ones.'

I can hear the birds singing their strongest songs to welcome the dark and let morning know they'll be waiting for it.

'She said "Oscar" for a joke. I'm really glad I didn't kick for that. It could have been so much worse. And then she tried "Wilde". It was a joke again, Dad said, but I kicked. Every time she said it, I kicked again. So, I chose my own name really. Sometimes I wish I hadn't, but I'm glad she gave me the chance.'

The calm, green dappled light filters the amber outside. I feel as if I'm floating.

'I never told anyone that before.'

'It is such a good name and such a good story.' Dorcas is very grave and thoughtful. Perhaps she has her own name story.

'Why are you called Dorcas?'

'Absolutely no idea.'

We burst out laughing.

'I'd better get back. While we can still see our way down the ladder.'

'Fairy lights. I'll get some.'

'Yes. And ribbons. I know they won't help us to see but they'd look so pretty. Imagine them fluttering in the breeze.'

If there ever is a breeze.

'See you at school tomorrow then.'

'Yes. See you then.'

I go out on to the platform and watch her till she's out of sight. Mae and Jules are sitting with their feet up in the kitchen and the donkey is taking a stroll around the garden.

I climb down the ladder and wander around, imagining how vibrant it must have been here when they staged a performance. Filled with people and laughter. I can see where the actors would enter and say their lines. The archway through the bushes as an entrance and the area around the treehouse as a stage. Then maybe the actors would have mingled with the audience, in character. I picture the bright costumes and the actors' words being caught like ornaments in the trees and bushes. I wonder what my mum's voice was like. If I sound like her.

Dorcas thought the story about my mum was interesting. Perhaps it is.

It's alright here. In this new life, there is hope.

4

'Argh!'

I wake up on the roof. Scrabble my heels against slate. Try not to fall. I grip as tight as I can to the tiles and feel the pull in my muscles, the crack as my bones pull.

What on earth am I doing up here? How did I get here? This is insane. It can't really be happening? It's impossible. I must be dreaming.

But I'm not. I'm on the roof, fighting for my life.

I try not to look down. I try not to panic. I panic. My heart races and I want to scream, but I'm afraid who might hear me.

'Help.' I whisper it into the tiles. Hope the house will somehow carry the sound down to Mae. It doesn't.

Concentrate. I manage to get a better grip on the slope. No one is coming to help. I need to do this on my own.

I'm lying flat on my front, so I inch my way breathlessly across the still hot slates and make it to the chimney. I am sweating and I feel sick rise in my throat. But I make it. Hugging on to the chimney, I try to get my breath back. To work out what's happening.

The moon is a light lime green. I concentrate on it to quell the dizziness. Sweat blurs my vision. I steady myself and reach a pyjama'd arm to wipe it from my eyes. Below me is death if I fall from this height. I need a plan.

Wait here till morning?

And be seen by the entire town and all the kids on their way to school?

I get up the guts to look down and feel vertigo twist inside me. It's a really long way.

If I got up here, then there must be a way down. I just need to think clearly.

I focus on the garden below me. Dark unknown things stretch and shudder the grass.

This must be a nightmare. I bite the inside of my mouth. 'Ow!' It's real.

Up here it is seriously scary. But…

I surprise myself with the 'but'.

But … once you get past that, it's magical.

Thrilling. It's just me. The flittering bats, the warm-porridge moon, and the air clear and full of possibility. No one knows I'm here. There's only the night and me. Up here, I can see like a bird. I am alone and free. I imagine sprouting wings. From beneath my shoulder blades, majestic and blooming. An eagle. A magnificent, powerful golden eagle.

What was that?

A shriek? A screech owl. Or perhaps a fox?

Breathe. Gulp my heart back down from my ears in a hard swallow. Ouch.

Again the shriek. Another electric surge of panic radiates through me.

I grip tight as a ghost owl lands next to me on the peak of the roof. It hooks the house with its talons. If I dared to let go, I could touch the owl's feathers. Stroke its head.

'I agree. It is beautiful,' I whisper to it, even though I'm as shaken as a baby's rattle. The weathervane moans its answer. The owl abandons me.

I shouldn't be up here. I should be in bed. My skylight is on the opposite side of the roof. I need to get to that or my bedroom window. If I go for the window, I will have to shimmy down and dangle over, holding the guttering while I try to swing my way in. Doesn't sound a brilliant option. The skylight will be easier.

Using the chimney, I heave myself up and peer over. I left the skylight open earlier, because Mae lets bats use it to come in and out. Getting to it is not going to be easy, but it's my best horrendous option.

I let go of the chimney, break out in flashes of sweat all over my body, and grab it again.

Come on, Wilde. You can do this.

I straddle the ridge, keeping the chimney at my back. Inch my legs over so that I am sitting as if ready to slide down.

Don't even think of it.

Pressing my feet hard into the roof tiles, I shuffle down the slope a tiny bit. I can do this. I edge a tiny bit further. Stop for breath. Edge a bit more. I have to do this slowly. I'll be killed if I fall. Stone dead. The fear gives me sharp focus.

Another inch. Down. It's so high. The skylight isn't so far away now. Another inch.

'Argh!' An owl swoops low and I skid, send some grit rattling down into the gutter. I claw wildly, my heart in my mouth. Drag myself to a stop on a patch where a slate is missing. Can't breathe. Deep gulps.

The skylight is close. One last effort. With my eyes so wide I am hardly blinking, I edge down a bit more. Prepared for the swoop of owls this time. Eventually, I make it to the skylight. Dangle my legs through its open mouth and rest for a second. The drop from here is going to hurt, but it's nothing compared to the fall I might have had.

My arms are tired, but I try to support myself so that I can dangle as low as possible before letting go. I still land with a thud and hurt my elbow and knee. But I'm alive.

Shaking all over, I get to my bed somehow. I climb straight in and pull the covers up over my head.

How did I get up there? I wrack my brain but there is no logical explanation. I don't believe in curses, but I do believe in weird. The weirdness has followed me here. This time I don't know if I can control it. It's worse than it has ever been before. Now it is getting dangerous.

5

'Why don't you have a normal clock?' Mae has bought a new clock with a photo of Tom Jones, a singer she adores, in the centre of it. Instead of chiming the hour it says 'Yeah' in a deep Welsh voice. 'I can hear that from my room, and it makes it pretty hard to sleep.'

'Oh, dear. Someone woke up on the wrong side of the bed.'

I don't tell her someone actually woke up on the roof, but I keep up my grump. I'm not good when I'm tired. Dad isn't good when he's tired either. He ranges from irritable to 'time to ignore him until he's had a nap'. I am at that point, where it's best to ignore me.

A goat trots into the kitchen. Mae gives the goat a carrot. 'This is Helen. Helen, this is Wilde.'

Helen bleats her version of a 'hello', then takes her carrot outside.

'It's not normal to have a goat in your house.'

'Says who?'

'Says me.'

'Then you must be right.' Mae raises an irritating eyebrow then chops up some coriander for a soup. 'How's the play going?'

'It's OK, thanks. It's not my sort of thing.' I spritz my hair with one of Mae's flower sprays and am horrified when it makes me smell like someone's nana.

'Patchouli, geranium and orange blossom. It's a calming mix which will keep its scent all day.'

Gutted to the nth degree.

'Well, let's just hope the play doesn't dredge up things which are better left forgotten.'

'I shouldn't think it will even dredge up an audience.'

'It's not a good topic to cover. There's too much emotion attached. And that Frocks Rutherford woman, or whatever her name is supposed to be, shouldn't be meddling with things that are none of her beeswax.'

'It happened a million years ago, Mae.'

'Places store memories. The things they did to those people, they seep into the roots of a town and poison it.'

'It's just made up. It's not like we are exhuming any bodies.' I don't know why I'm not agreeing with Mae. I don't want to do a play about witches. I'm just in a grouchy mood so ready for an argument.

'Your mum wouldn't have let you take part.'

The world freezes. Mae never talks about my mum anymore. I don't say anything. Wait for her to carry on. She doesn't.

'My mum loved drama, didn't she?'

'Yes. She loved theatre, but she wouldn't have liked the subject matter. She was different. Talented. Like you. She could see things.'

It's difficult to get my words out. 'What do you mean? See things?'

'In glass. In water. The future. The past. Scrying, it's called.'

'Whatever that is, I don't believe in it.' I don't want to believe in it because I'm doing my best to be normal. 'I don't believe in it AT ALL,' I say, for good measure.

'Then I must be making it up.' Mae briskly attacks the sink with a scouring pad. 'Whatever you believe, young lady, this town used to try witches and hang them, and we shouldn't be making light of it.'

'That's horrible.'

'Yes, it is.'

I feel the creeps, thick and threatening. How did I get on to the roof? Nothing like that has ever happened to me before.

Mrs Danvers comes in and sly-eyes me to show me she knows everything. She leaves with a very smug twitch of her tail.

I don't like this conversation. But I need to know more. It's like picking a scab. I need to know everything.

'"The Witch called Winter" is just a story, Mae.'

'Is it?'

'You really believe in it?' I am scared now, but pretending to be incredulous. 'All of it?'

'Yes, I really do.' Mae scrubs harder. 'Your dad doesn't like me talking to you about this.'

I wait. Is she finally going to tell me what is wrong with me? Tell me properly about Mum? The smell of patchouli steams up from my clothes.

'Forget I said anything…'

'But…'

'No. My lips are sealed.' She hurries out into the garden.

I go upstairs to get my school bag. Looking out of the witch window, I squint into the sun. My mum gazed out of this window once upon a time.

She could do unusual things. I am unusual.

I examine the skylight. There's no way I could have got up through it. I must have gone out through the witch window.

Mrs Danvers barges her way into my room and lies down in the most inconvenient central spot.

'You could tell me all about her, couldn't you, Mrs Danvers?'

She considers me with her odd-coloured eyes, then licks her bits to mark her indifference. She wouldn't have met my mum, but she's eavesdropped on all Mae's conversations over the years. She knows what my mum could do. What she was and why Dad is trying to hide it. Why won't Mae tell me more? She is so annoying.

I go and brush my teeth, hard. Tie my plaits tightly so I won't have to do them again. Get my mind set for another day of being The Same at school. Hoisting the backpack Mae has given me over my shoulders, I stomp downstairs. It's not fair that everyone knows more about my mum than I do. It's not fair that they all keep secrets. If anyone should know things about her, then it should be me. I slam the door on my way out.

I stride to the end of our road. Sun glare strains my eyes. Cars. Fumes. Engines growling. I turn the corner to the school.

Brakes screeching. No laughter. No shouting. Children staring. Parents staring. Everyone staring. I realise that the sun is no longer shining on me. I am completely shaded.

Looking up, I see an undulating cloud of starlings. Thousands of them, making black waves in the sky.

Wow. It's amazing.

The starlings start to swoop low, around me, almost catching at the ends of my plaits. I try to walk calmly through the gate, but they follow. I have to run.

I stop at the school entrance. *Go away, please.* Squeezing my eyes tight shut, I think of waterfalls, calm places. Fish circling under ripples of watery light. The moon-path on the sea.

I open my eyes and they are gone.

Everyone is staring at me now. Pointing fingers. I don't know what's happening. I'm scared. Really scared. I push through the doors, dash past the receptionist and his too-big teeth. Run past the pictures of witches and freaks. Get to our classroom, which is empty, and slump into my seat. Putting my head down on my desk, I try to process everything.

Now everyone will think I'm afraid of birds and make fun of me. I should have stayed home. Mae shouldn't have made me come to this school in the first place. I'll go. I'll get my registration mark and go. Except I don't want Jemima to think I was too scared of the birds to stay. Why should the bully win again? I'll see the day through.

I think about Dad. I need him to come back now. Why can't I go and join him in Massachusetts? I've always wanted to go to America.

The door opens and someone comes in. I keep my head down. The someone is crying. I have to look.

It's Susan Stevens. I haven't spoken to her properly. She sits down at her desk with a note in her hands. I don't know if she's noticed me.

'Are you okay?' I ask.

She jumps, thrusts the note in her drawer and hugs herself.

'I'm Wilde. I've never really spoken to you. I'm

sorry. I find it difficult to introduce myself to people.'

I walk over and sit next to her. I may as well be nice, before I leave here forever. What have I got to lose?

'You don't have to tell me, but I'm here if you need someone. At least, I'm here today anyway.'

She doesn't make eye contact. I bet she's been at the end of Jemima's whip-like tongue more than a few times.

'I'll go now. But if you need me, I am just here.'

I get up, but she grasps my arm. I sit back down. She gets the note out of her drawer and holds it in front of her. It trembles.

'Can I read it?'

She sniffles.

'I won't tell anyone. I promise.'

She gives it to me. She is shaking so much I can barely catch hold of it. I unfold the note. It's written in green ink.

'Susan Stevens, your secret is out. I know your terrible history and it is about to catch up with you. You are cursed. THE WITCH.'

Mr Ricketts comes in with a cacophony of children in his wake.

'Sir, did you see that?' Lewis hurls his satchel across the classroom, and it slides off and spews its contents onto the floor. 'It was awesome.'

'Take a seat, please, Lewis.'

The other kids arrive in various states of hysteria. Mr Ricketts picks at chewing gum stuck to his shoe while he gives a lecture on the horrors of all things chewed and sticky and the various places he has discovered them.

THE WITCH? I'm shaking.

I move back to my seat. Susan is so upset. I can see her shoulders slumped and her head hanging low.

Why is everything about witches? Who wrote that note to her?

The room is full of whispering. My stomach's an airborne pancake.

It comes out of my mouth without warning. Sulphurous orange vomit, like lava. It hits Lewis's bag. It's over quickly, but the reaction isn't. Shrieks. Ewws. Shouts. People acting like they are going to be sick themselves. Laughs hidden behind hands. Mr Ricketts calling for paper towels. Mopping. I run out of the classroom.

The girls' toilet is empty. I lock myself in a

cubicle and lean my head against the door. What is happening with the birds? The crow in my lap. The owl on the roof. The starlings. So many birds. Waking up on the roof? And now, as if all that wasn't too much to cope with, THE WITCH.

Someone comes in. I wish I could disappear.

'Wilde?' It's Dorcas. 'Are you alright?'

It's pointless hiding. She won't give up. I already know she's like that. I slide the latch on the door then go straight to wash my hands and splash water on my face.

'It's probably the heat. It can make you really poorly. Dehydration. Lots of people died in a heatwave in America in 1936 because they jumped into waterways to cool down even though they couldn't swim. They drowned, obviously. Worth bearing in mind.'

I press my wet fingertips to my eyelids. 'How do you know this stuff?'

'I am interested in everything. For example, I read about how the Victorians used to take photos of their dead loved ones as if they were still alive. I'm a bit nervous about going to Witch Point High, everyone is, but I want to do a presentation next year about it, using my new Year Seven form teacher as a corpse if they'll agree. I've had a chat with the caretaker, Stanley, about saving the environment and he says he has swapped his usual cleaning products for all homemade natural ones to help, which is brilliant and means he doesn't have to wear rubber gloves, which make his hands smell like dead rats. I saw a butterfly on the way into school and when I pointed to it, it came and landed on my finger, probably because I'd had sugar puffs for breakfast and ate them without a spoon. And that murmuration of starlings, swooping so low and so close. That's not how they usually behave. All the birds are acting peculiarly.'

'Well, it's nothing to do with me,' I snap.

'Wilde. I know you are feeling ill, but you must be feeling sick to the maximum if you think any of it has anything to do with you!' She laughs.

I glance at her.

'I just mean that everything is going nuts in this weather. It's exhausting. My mum said last night she had to put frozen sprouts in her pillowcase. No one really wants to eat them anyway, so it didn't matter.'

We start walking to class. Dorcas offers me a mint while she talks.

'...and that's why I told Mum that her only option was to put all our clothes in the freezer.'

We have Page to Stage this morning, so we go to the hall. Lewis passes me my bag.

'Thank you. I'm sorry about yours.'

'Don't worry. My baby brother was sick on it last night as well. Mr Ricketts cleaned that off too. Result.'

He is easily pleased.

6

'Into a circle, please, young people. Into a circle. That's it. Into a circle.' Gwyneth Fox-Rutherford spends ages rounding us up and even then everyone apart from me keeps talking. 'Superlative. We are now enclosed in a circle of trust.'

She looks directly at me and then straight up into the sky. I think she is checking for birds. She must have seen the starlings earlier. I'm glad she looks up; it gives me an excuse to do the same.

Nothing. The sun roasts white overhead and, apart from a buzzard a very long way off, there is nothing to fear.

'The curse!' Gwyneth proclaims dramatically. I snap my head to look at her. It doesn't have the same effect on anyone else. They all keep yapping and straggling out of shape.

'Can we have some quiet, please, guys? Quiet, please. I said, SHUT UP.' Gwyneth's eyes bulge. I think she's surprised herself by losing her temper so quickly.

'We aren't allowed to use those words, miss. They are extremely rude.' Jemima's eyes are wide with horror. She really is quite the actor.

'Apologies, folks. It's the heat. Making me a little short-tempered. But now I have your attention, may our journey into the unknown past commence.'

Gwyneth does a little jig of celebration. Someone yawns loudly. To be fair it is pretty difficult to concentrate in this heat.

'Excellent start. Yawning is good for relaxation and allowing our bodies to be refreshed and in the moment. Join me in awakening our conscious selves.' She yawns. Everyone joins in yawning, long and hard and way, way, way too loud. Lewis, back from a brief spell in Time Out, is walking a thin line already.

'Wonderful.'

Lewis yawns again and makes everyone laugh. Gwyneth pretends to take it on the chin and smiles a patronising smile. 'Are we ready?'

Lewis yawns a tiny yawn. This time Gwyneth doesn't even pretend to smile.

'We are going to start with, what I like to call the "actor warm-up". She makes inverted commas in the air and uses a voice which she clearly thinks is funny. I don't really get it, but I don't want this woman to feel embarrassed. Just because she's an adult it doesn't mean life's easy.

'I don't think we need to warm up, Miss. It's boiling.'

'Jemima Morgan, is it?'

'How do you know my name?'

'I'm keeping my eye on you.'

Jemima preens. 'I'm glad, Miss, because I'm really good at Drama.'

'Wonderful. Now, please don't call me Miss. Call me Gwyneth.'

A ripple of laughter.

'Gwyneth.' Lewis tests it out and gets a laugh again.

'The first part of the warm-up is to shake your faces like this.' She clasps her hands together and shakes her head loosely. Some of the class copy her with so much energy that there is a danger of their heads falling off. I do it half-heartedly, so I won't mess up my plaits. She makes us pretend we have a busy bee on our fingertip, waving it around while we make a buzzing noise; do an impression of a horse, which makes my lips tingle; and sing lots of la's back to her. Gwyneth loves every minute of it. I don't.

By the time we finish the warm-up, we are struggling to breathe, it's so hot, and we are instructed to sit in the shade of the willow tree. Gwyneth looks panicked by the state of us. She's not a teacher so I guess she doesn't think about health and safety. Even in this willowy green tangle, the sun has lemoned the grass, but it's heavenly after the piercing bright of the yard.

We sip from our forever bottles and wait. Even Lewis is too hot to cause trouble.

Gwyneth unwinds her sparkly neck-scarf and sits on the grass cross-legged. 'The curse!'

She looks at me. I look at Susan Stevens. Susan Stevens stares solidly at Gwyneth and refuses to catch my eye.

'The curse on this town was put here by a horrible, terrible witch.'

I shrink into myself.

'I am about to tell you the tale of the evil witch they named Winter!'

'Heard it.' Lewis has recovered.

'Ah, little boy, but you haven't heard my version.'

The class scoff at her attempt to humiliate. I want to tell her she's just being nasty because he spoiled her moment.

She lowers her voice and, despite the heat, we are caged in this emerald world and her words charm us.

'In the middle of Witch Point woods, centuries ago, there was a humble cottage. A woodcutter and his wife lived there with their seven daughters. Beautiful were their daughters. Kind and true.'

She looks around, eyeballing us to make sure she has our attention. She does. Everyone loves creepy stories, even when they've heard them a million times.

'One fateful night, a witch came upon that humble cottage and peering through the windows saw the happiness of the family who sat by candlelight inside. The wicked witch wanted to kill their love stone *dead*, so bitter was she.'

Gwyneth punches her own leg for emphasis on the word 'dead'. You can tell it hurts her, but she doesn't stop.

'The evil, pus-covered hag put an enchantment on herself to disappear her pimples, vanish her pustules and make the fleas which crawled from her ears jump off her skin and look for others' blood on which to feed.'

This is gross, but everyone except for me and Susan seems to be loving it.

'She cast a bewitchment on herself, to make her look like a lonely and destitute girl. When the family sat in front of their meagre fire to eat, she crossed their poor threshold and sat down at their pitiful, scrap-filled table.' Gwyneth acts this all out, wrapping the willow fronds around her like rags.

'"Who are you?" the woodcutter demanded,' Gwyneth booms in a deep, stern voice, throwing the leaves aside and putting her fist up, ready to fight.

'"I am but a poor and meek and destitute girl, Sir," the witch replied.' Gwyneth is all innocence and wringing hands.

'"Let us take her in, poor little wren," the woodcutter's wife cried.' In a very shrill voice, apparently.

'"Oh yes! We would so love an eighth sister!

Please, father!'" Gwyneth gets a bit carried away here, trying to portray ten different characters at once. I am worn out just watching her.

'The witch wormed her way into the family's affections and trouble came soon enough.'

We all lean in.

'One night, as the snow began to fall, the witch convinced the sisters that they should all come with her through the woods "to a place of great beauty". Being trusting and good through and through, they followed her out into the woods. Soon the blizzard became so thick they couldn't see their path home. She lured them to where the seven rivers meet, at the Falls of Snow waterfall, and there she drowned them in revenge for all the witches who had been dunked and drowned before her. They haunt the rivers forever.'

Gwyneth gives a theatrical cackle to end.

I don't feel well. This story of the witch – it feels wrong. My heart thuds painfully. Something twangs my memory, out of reach. I try really hard to remember, but it's cloudy and I can't get to it.

'What does dunked mean, miss?'

'It means the witches were held underwater to

see if they would cast a spell to save themselves. If they drowned, they weren't witches. If they lived, then they were.'

'That's stupid.'

'Thank you, Lewis.'

Dorcas pipes up. 'They did other things to them too. Rolled them down hills in barrels filled with spikes. Burned them at the stake. They crushed them with huge stones to get false confessions. They even killed their pets if they were thought to have helped with witchcraft.'

'That's enough, thank you, Dorcas.'

'What happened to the witch called Winter, Miss?'

'She was caught by a witch hunt and hanged for her hideous crimes. As she swung from the noose by her neck, she left an evil curse on the poor town and its people so that everyone would have bad luck forever. An everlasting curse on Witch Point.'

The class has heard this legend before, but they're still excited to hear such a dramatic rendition. I feel as if I'm going to be sick again. By the look on Susan's face, she feels the same.

'She sounds like a really horrible witch,' Jemima

says, smiling spitefully at me. 'We are extremely proud of our heritage here, Miss. When will auditions be, Miss? I mean, Gwyneth.'

Jemima is all angelic golden-halo hair and I feel my face crease like a raisin.

'We have the rest of the day to cast. I have these for you.' She hands out photocopies of the script. 'Practise. Auditions shall begin anon.'

Dorcas pipes up, 'Which could be an abbreviation of anonymous but in this context means soon.'

'Thank you, Dorcas.'

'I'm completely ready, Gwyneth,' Jemima smugs as she has never smugged before.

'One is never completely ready, Jemima. One can always improve.'

I feel a nasty sense of satisfaction as Jemima turns ketchup red from her neck to her fringe.

'Ten minutes of preparation, then let battle commence!'

People busy themselves with their audition pieces. I sulk on my own and pretend to be reading through lines: 'I am a terrible witch. A hideous hag. I am ruthless and heartless, and I hang my head in shame.'

I can hear Jemima projecting the same lines loudly outside the curtain of leaves. They suit her.

I'm going to let Gwyneth know that I'd like to help with directing, scriptwriting, stage management, or anything offstage, but before I get a chance she goes to get some more water from the canteen and leaves us on our own, which I'm pretty certain is Not Allowed.

'That was very weird, wasn't it, girls?'

The Sleeks come through the willow curtain on cue and move in my direction.

'All those birds in one place.'

'And when *she* went inside, they all disappeared.'

'As if she could control them or something.'

'A witch could do that. Control things.'

'A real witch.' Holly and Ivy burst out laughing.

'Stay well away from her.' Jemima's voice is glacial. 'Careful, don't go too close. She might put a spell on you.'

The twins shriek away, laughing and pretending to be zombies. Jemima glides away, a swan made of ice. I hear anger fizzing in my ears.

'Hang the witch,' someone shouts. The floor swoops beneath me.

Gwyneth comes back into the wavering green looking less than pleased. 'Right, Year Six. Come and sit down.'

Everyone carries on as if she hasn't said anything.

'Come and SIT DOWN, I said.'

Everyone sits. Except Lewis, who carries on rehearsing his lines until he notices, about a minute later, that everyone is smirking at him.

'See, Miss Gwyneth? That's why I should have the main part. I've already got an audience, haven't I?' He bows and everyone cheers.

Gwyneth takes out a huge folder and puts on some thick-rimmed black glasses. Auditions start. There's no way I'm auditioning. I want to work backstage, then at least no one will be looking at me.

When the hilarity of the first few auditions is over, it becomes a bit boring. Dorcas's very enthusiastic reading brings me out of my stupor for a bit. I am forced to stumble through a couple of lines. Jemima takes herself way too seriously, but is irritatingly good. A couple of the others make a decent job of it, but my attention is waning fast.

When Mum and Mae used to put on plays, it was for fun. They used every inch of the garden as a theatre and invited friends and relatives. One year, the year Dad fell in love with Mum, they put on *A Midsummer Night's Dream* and floated candles on the pond and strung fairy lights in the trees. Dad says he was as enchanted by my mum as if he had really had the love-in-idleness flower squeezed into his eyes by a meddlesome fairy.

They stuck with Shakespeare because it was so successful; with Mum and Mae playing lots of roles at all their garden parties. Mum didn't want to do it professionally, so when Mae went off to drama college, she stayed behind and was a seamstress. She was planning to do a PhD on Shakespeare with the Open University. She never did in the end. I wonder if she would have had a more exciting life if she hadn't settled down with Dad and had me. I wonder if she would have gone off and seen the world like I'm going to. If she could foresee things like Mae said, did she know what was going to happen to her? Could she see the future me?

Eventually, Gwyneth gives us a two-minute break while she casts. I stay in the same spot, so I won't have to chat to anyone. I try not to think about all the things that have happened lately. I try to empty my mind, like they taught us to do in mindfulness breaks in my last school. Instead of emptying, my brain immediately fills with a tsunami of thoughts, curses, screams, vicious claws grabbing for me, and birds, millions of birds, taking me up into the sky, then dropping me like a stone.

Gwyneth claps her hands.

'It's been a difficult job casting. Each and every one of you was superb in your own way.' She paces the stage area. 'I've tried to be fair and give an accurate reflection of talent, ability and commitment, whilst also suiting the person to the role as creatively and cleverly as is humanly possible.'

We sit and wait.

'"A Witch called Winter" – the cast!' She lists the parts. Ivy is cast as Winter and stands to punch the air. Holly is one of the seven. Lewis gets the part of the woodcutter and asks if that means he can have a real axe. He's told no. Dorcas is the woodcutter's wife, which she looks happy with. Lewis asks if that means they have to argue all the time. He's told no. The others are all given parts they seem content with. Even Susan Stevens smiles.

'Wilde, you will be the hangman.'

I put my hand up shakily. 'Miss, I don't want to be onstage. I'd like to help direct or…'

'Impossible, I'm afraid. We need everyone to take part. The executioner will be your role.'

'But, Miss, I don't feel comfortable onstage.' Or with being the executioner.

'Then I will give you some extra tuition.' Her eyes are magnified by her glasses.

I put my hand down. I don't want extra tuition. I don't want to be in the play.

I'll be off sick. I'll explain to Mae that it's all too stressful for me. She'll understand and if she doesn't, I'll hide. Or I'll drink saltwater to make myself throw up. I've done it before, it's not that bad.

A thin, hesitant voice calls out. 'Miss.' It's Jemima. 'You didn't call me out.'

'Ah, yes. What's your name again?'

'Jemima, Miss. You said you were keeping an eye on me, Miss. I mean, Gwyneth.'

Jemima is visibly shaking. Her face is taut, her cheeks pinched. This is really, really unfair.

'Erm.' Gwyneth scans through her list a few times, then takes her pen from behind her ear and writes. 'Third woodcutter from the left.'

Even I can see that is wrong. Jemima may be a horrible person, but she shines when she is acting. A light glows inside her.

Gwyneth snaps her folder shut triumphantly and sweeps out, beckoning to us to follow. 'Exit pursued by a bear.'

We all get up except Jemima, who sits for a moment too long. My heart goes out to her. I know what it's like to want something so badly and not be able to have it. I can imagine that throbbing feeling she must have in her throat. Holly and Ivy are whispering and glancing over at her. She straightens her back and stands.

'Stupid play, anyway.' She heads away from school. I chase after her, her ponytail bobbing ahead of me.

'Jemima.'

She ignores me, walking briskly.

'Jemima.'

She stops and turns, tears streaking her face.

'You can have my part if you want. I really don't want it.'

'How kind of you to give me your cast-offs.'

'I don't mean it like that. I'd rather not be in the play at all. Honestly. I'm not being nasty. It's just…' It's impossible to give her my part. I should have known she'd be humiliated by the offer. 'I just. I want you to have it. Please. You'd be doing me a favour.'

She seems uncertain for a second, then looks over my shoulder to Holly and Ivy on the far side of the yard. They are still whispering. Jemima glowers at me and now there's no uncertainty in her eyes. There's just plain hatred.

'You are weird. So weird. My mother knew your mother and she told me what you are.'

I don't answer. Hate is searing, the smell of it like singed grass.

'She said that you can put curses on people.'

There's a vacuum of air between us, like we are stuck inside a bubble. It's too hot. Burning from the inside out. Burning from the outside in.

'That it runs in the family. That you are a witch. That your mother was a witch.'

I wish the bubble could float me away.

I close my eyes and imagine taking flight. Soaring up, the school tiny below me. Floating on thermals.

Bursting through the clouds in glimmering sparkles. Sunlight kisses my wings, glitters, trails behind me in shimmering waves. I am a part of the air and the sky, and light as a feather.

When I open my eyes, Jemima is gone. The school is empty. I am alone.

7

I've had a terrible night's sleep again. When I arrive at school, I can tell things are worse. Jemima and a few of the others are whispering and lots of kids stare at me as I pass. A minibus crammed with Year Fives is departing for a day on a beach and I imagine sneaking myself in as a stowaway. I don't think I could get away with it. Dorcas is hurtling towards me at top speed across the yard.

'Have you heard? There have been lots of curses left overnight.'

I feel cold creep over me.

'Mabli Evans had one that said she would grow bunions so big that she wouldn't be able to dance anymore, and she lives for dancing. Megan had a curse that if she took another photo of herself, she'd grow hair all over her face like a wolf, and taking selfies is literally her only hobby.' Dorcas is out of breath but carries on. 'There was one in Cadi's desk and Lewis found one inside his bag, but he couldn't read it because his baby brother had been sick in it again. I...'

'Who were they signed from?'

'The Witch. Have you had one?'

'No.'

'Nor me. There've been all sorts of sightings and rumours. People think that we've woken the witch called Winter. That she has come back from the grave. That she's cursed us all over again, but stronger this time. That there are even more horrors to come.'

'Ridiculous.' My voice struggles to get past my lips. It doesn't believe itself.

As we walk to class, I can see people reading each other's notes. I pass Ivy as she finds one white-tacked to her locker and bursts into tears. She crumples it up and refuses to show it to anyone, even to Holly, so it must be bad.

This is terrible. Really terrible. When we get to class, it gets worse. Mr Ricketts has been taken into hospital, so we have to go straight to Gwyneth for registration.

'What's wrong with him?' I ask the secretary,

but he doesn't hear me because he is dealing with Branwen's asthma inhaler. Lewis butts in.

'He's been cursed. My mam saw him being taken away in an ambulance and she said he was being sick more than my baby brother is and that is a heck of a lot, let me tell you.'

I feel the tingle of tears at the bridge of my nose.

The others head off to the hall in a state of high excitement. Ivy is telling everyone about her note without revealing the contents. Jemima's nose is out of joint as she's not getting the attention. She narrows her eyes at me and I know that our encounter yesterday is not over yet.

I lag behind, realising too late that setting myself apart from the group probably makes me more suspicious.

Someone human must be writing those notes. Trying to cause trouble. For me. For everyone. I know bad things happen around me, but I didn't make anyone ill.

Unless?

No. I'm not cursing people. I'm not writing the curses.

Unless, you are doing it in your sleep.

I am not doing it in my sleep.

The illustration of the witch called Winter in the corridor is lit by a shaft of glittering sunlight. I stop to look at it. Something still feels not right about it. Why did the Page to Stage production have to be about witches? Why couldn't we have had a summer fayre like other schools, with fairy cakes and candy-floss and perhaps a mini Ferris wheel? Or a play based on literally anything else?

Something moves in the glass frame, but when I peer closer I realise it's the receptionist behind me.

'Come along. Get to class.' He holds a Witch Point folder tightly. He must have files on every pupil. I don't like him knowing all that information about me. I wonder if he has information on my mum in his archives. Is that why he's always watching me?

I have no choice but to walk with him. When we get to the hall, Gwyneth is doing some peculiar yoga moves and grunting.

'A salutation to the sun,' she explains and continues to contort herself into surprising shapes. She loves an audience and having the receptionist there gives extra flamboyance to her moves.

Jemima shoves past me, hurting my shoulder, and goes towards Gwyneth. 'Did you hear, Gwyneth? The witch is back and cursing everyone.'

Everyone gasps. We aren't telling the teachers. Jemima is breaking the unspoken Year Six code.

Gwyneth stops yoga-ing and puts her glasses on. 'Is that so?'

'It is so.' Jemima is thoroughly pleased with herself. It makes me want to punch her. I loosen my collar and still feel as if I'm being throttled. There should be a law to close schools in this heat.

'Winter has come to wreak her revenge at last.' Gwyneth looks over her shoulder. 'We must tread with care, my company of players, for we do not want to upset the spirits.'

It's clear that Gwyneth thinks Jemima is making things up to get a role in the play, but she's happy to play along with the theatricality of it. Everyone mutters about spirits and curses. The air is bubbling with expectation, on a knife-edge of nerves. I bet none of us are sleeping in this heat.

'ARGHHHHHHHHHH!' Gwyneth screams. We all scream in response. 'Twisted my ankle. Sorry, everyone.'

All I can hear is people murmuring 'curse'. One girl starts crying and dashes out of the room.

'What a darling, caring so much for my pain.' Gwyneth hobbles to sit on the edge of the stage. The class babbles with excitement and shock. 'Fear not, for I am fine, my merry band of vagabonds.'

More whispers. Everything is curse, curse, curse.

'This is just stupid,' I say, louder than I mean to. Everyone stares at me. 'Everyone is just getting freaked out by the heat.'

'You can, I suppose, blame our uneasiness on the heatwave, Wilde. You can blame our unsettled feelings on coincidence. But the accidents...' Gwyneth rubs her ankle. 'The effect it's having on our minds – perhaps we should abandon the project, go back to class and let dead witches lie.'

Huge moan from the others. Someone spits a paper pellet at me, which is gross. They're worried we'll have to do work instead. I wish we could. The sun beats through the window. My heart hammers. I think I'm going to faint, but Susan steadies me.

'No!' Gwyneth bellows. 'We shall not give in to

her archaic sorcery. We shall go into battle and use theatre as our weapon! We must show everyone the story of this evil witch to expose her and stop the everlasting curse on Witch Point now!' She bays a battle cry, as if she is commanding an evil spectre out of the room.

My world twirls, I stagger and I'm sent to sit alone in the shade like an outcast.

The others rehearse even more vigorously, afraid of being struck down too. I sit with my head between my knees until I've managed to stem my tears.

When I look up, faces of hate are around me. The mob are waving imaginary pitchforks and chanting 'Hang her' over and over. Their mouths are angry slashes and their words are filled with fire. I put my head back between my knees and press my ears shut.

Finally, the session is over. Gwyneth tells us the school will be sending out ticket sales details and we leave. A dark cloud hangs over us, filled with fear and spite.

The rest of the day goes by. We have taster sessions for what next year will be like at Witch Point High with teachers visiting us from the secondary school. Everyone is nervous about moving up, even if they are pretending they aren't. An English teacher comes in to take us for a silent walk and we have to make a list of everything we notice with our senses. Then there is a P.E. taster where I watch from the sidelines because I still feel queasy and I don't have any kit. Then there's a too-short History taster where we research the Tower of London and all the beheadings there. When the teacher says that history is full of gory stuff and that, in Year Seven, we are going to be looking at Vlad the Impaler and his influence on the story of *Dracula*, I know we would get on if I went to Witch Point High. Which is a shame because I won't be going.

Eventually, it's home time and I can leave. I really like Dorcas, and some of the others in my class are nice too, but The Sleeks have been sly-eyeing me all day and I'm glad to escape.

It's so hot. My breath catches in my throat. Some of the others went swimming together last weekend. A waterfall not far from here. Sgŵd-yr-Eira – The Falls of Snow. I felt a delicious cold shiver when I heard them talking about it, because that's where the photo of my mum and me was taken. I realise it's in the story of Winter, too: it's where the seven rivers meet that are said to be the seven daughters, the waterfall where Winter is said to have trapped them. But the link between me and my mum is what calls to me. That's where I want to go right now. Right this second.

When I swim in Mumbles or the Gower, it always helps my worries. I front crawl them away. I can do that at the waterfall. It sounds so cold. I can imagine myself standing beneath it. The thought gets me home.

'Mae, I'm going swimming.'

There isn't any answer. I can't face the stairs. My swimming costume is at the top, but sweat trickles down my neck and soaks through the back of my shirt. I kick my shoes off, press the tiles with my feet and feel the cool of the house rise through me.

'Mae?' My voice echoes up the emptiness.

I need an ice-pop. It's so hot I can't think of anything but that waterfall and how I'm going to pack my forever bottle with ice cubes and rub them over my face on the way there.

As soon as I get a moment alone with the freezer, Mae dashes in from the conservatory.

'Are you OK, Mae?' She looks so worried.

'They are all dying.' Mae is close to tears. 'All of them. The flowers. It's the heat. We need to do something now.'

I can't say I was going to go swimming. The flowers are Mae's livelihood and love. Grabbing a tray of pots, I join her in the mad dash to get all her plants into the shady spot behind the house. It hardly gets the sun because it's surrounded by trees. There's a pond here. Something plops into it. I wouldn't mind getting in myself. Mae knows her flowers well, so we must be helping them by putting them here.

As we rush back and forth, the direct sunlight drives through my head like a laser, but I press on. I need to be there for Mae.

Eventually all the plants are in the shade and watered. I help her to spray their leaves and enjoy the mist kissing my skin. We flop down on the grass in a comfortable silence.

'Wilde. Are you happy here?'

The question comes from nowhere, so it takes me a minute to think how to answer. At this moment, I am very happy. Lying here on this sweet grass, surrounded by grateful flowers. I miss Dad but I'm due to speak to him again tomorrow and his work is very important. The stuff at school is difficult and most of the time I'm ragged from pretending to be normal but right now … 'Yes, I am.'

'I'm glad.' She lifts a ladybird gently on to a fragile pink petal. 'It's where you belong.'

I look up at the sky, way above us. Beyond the yellow whispering leaves, it is crystal bright. 'Can I sleep in the treehouse tonight?'

'Of course.'

Sometimes things I think will be difficult are really very easy.

I drag a few bits up the ladder with me. Mae helps. We sweep the worst of the debris away and, though it is hot work, it is nice to be with her. We even sing a song, a Welsh folk song we both know about different-coloured goats, and then a rap only I know. Mae joins in like a beatbox and, though it's out of time and we sound awful, it's really fun. By the time we finish, Mae is satisfied that I can sleep on the roll-down mattress she's found. I haven't told her about the curses, and sleepwalking, and ending up on the roof. Witch Point, for all its bad luck, is a very safe area where everyone knows everyone else so she has no worries about my safety. I have so many worries rattling about inside my head, I'm a human maraca.

Mae goes down and I sit on the platform for a bit, watching all the animals wombling around. The flowers shine their best colours as night begins to fall and their scents get heady as they try to attract the last of the day's insects. Hornets drone past as the sky bruises. The owls begin to call and I turn on my torch.

I can see Dorcas's house from here. I'm glad she lives so close. I wish she was staying over with me. Mae is reading a book in a rocking chair in her room. I signal her with the torch and she waves back. I go inside, making sure she witnesses me, and lie down on the mattress. It's a bit lumpy but I get comfy and open a book. It's a jolly thing with brightly-coloured illustrations and lots of bits of poems.

When day is spent, and bright sun's song is done,
The fair folk whirl the sky by gold moonlight.

As the dark grows, I think about The Witch. I imagine myself writing those letters in a trance. I couldn't have, could I? I don't know enough about the other pupils. Remembering this makes me feel a whole lot better. I try not to worry about what might happen if I fall asleep. What if I sleepwalk out of the treehouse and straight off the platform edge? Perhaps I should have asked to sleep in the conservatory. No, too hot. A tent in the garden? At least then I'd be on ground level.

Spell little ones with lullabies sweetly sung,
And everything is given to the night.

8

'Help!' I am way above the ground. My face is crushed into stone. *Get a grip.* It takes me a minute to believe where I am. The windmill on the edge of town? How did I get here? Sweat makes my hands slippery. My breathing is harsh, clawing. The night sky above me seems to want to lift me up. I cling to the solid comfort of stone.

What is happening? I can't have sleepwalked all the way here? What other explanation is there?

I'm going to have to tell someone about this. It's getting too dangerous. I don't want to tell Mae. She'd tell Dad and he'd worry.

I'll tell Dorcas. She'll know what to do.

The thought of Dorcas, my new friend, gives me the courage to sit up and look around. There's no one here. That's a relief.

I am so high. The windmill watches over the town from the top of Witch Point Hill. They said in class it's where they used to roll the witches in those spike-and-nail-filled barrels. Horrid. I look down and imagine how frightening it must have been.

Far away, I see my beloved sea glimmering in the distance. A spellbinding line of 'wish you were here'. Closer, the town wheezes irritably. I'm high up but I'm safe. I can sit here until I feel less shaky. I close my eyes and try to think why and how I could have got here. It makes no sense, but then I suppose, nothing makes much sense when you really look at it. Pearls disappear in vinegar. Elephants can't walk backwards. Sheep always turn uphill. Dorcas told me all these things.

This has got to stop happening. It's getting seriously, seriously weird.

Grasping onto the stone, I swing my legs inside the open-topped windmill. The missing roof means the steps down are easy to see and there is a doorway I can get out through. I don't need to rush now; I'm safe.

Dad told me once my mum spent days carving her initials into this ruin. Is that what brought me here? I wonder how hard it would be to find them. As I think this, I put my hand down to steady myself and feel something under my fingertips.

It can't be.

Roughly chiselled into the stone: Mum's initials. Mae would say it was fate.

My mum used to sit here. Play here. I feel such a strong connection to her. I know it sounds silly, but it's like she's trying to tell me something. I look about me. What is it? Something. Tugging at my memory. Like water slipping through my fingers. I'm sorry, Mum. I just can't catch it.

I trace the indents in the stone, concentrating on the rough, dusty patterns. I swallow hard and stay practical. Whatever I'm trying to pinpoint ghosts itself away.

I shuffle towards the steps. I need to make plans. Stop this sleepwalking before it stops me.

I cautiously make my way down the steps. It wouldn't be good to fall here – there are jagged points of glass where people have left broken bottles. Disgusting. I promise that I will clean this up soon, but in daylight. I reach the bottom safely and celebrate freedom.

In the baked darkness, the town slumbers in shadow pockets beneath the stars. Mae says it has been getting hotter and hotter since I arrived. There hasn't been a drop of rain in Witch Point for ages and everyone has had enough. Including me, even though I haven't been here that long. I remember rain. It was glorious. This might be a curse or it might be the climate crisis brought on by stupid humans.

The ground is warm beneath my bare feet. It has to be the weather causing the sleepwalking. It's never happened to me before. I stop to let a critter cross the path ahead of me. A rat or a weasel. It's probably searching for water, poor thing.

Attempting to ignore my sore soles, I descend the steps to the sliding cemetery and hobble past a tilted grave. It is on the outside of the wall, turned to face the wrong way. A witch maybe?

Through the kissing gate and over the lane, using all my willpower to keep walking. Bats flitting. Owls crying. Down the rickety path home where Mrs Danvers welcomes me by turning her bum in my direction.

'Charming.' I'm so happy to have made it back in one piece I almost hug her.

I don't want to go back to the treehouse. I want

to be close to the ground. The hallway is a sickly blue. I creep into one of the *Sleepy Hollow* chairs in the drawing room and curl up tight. I must not sleep again until I've solved this. I try telling lies to sting me awake.

'I'm not worried.'

Lie.

'I'm not afraid that there is something wrong with me.'

Lie.

'I am not a witch because witches don't exist and so it's simply impossible.'

Lie. Lie. Lie.

Alone, I watch the milky sunlight pink into yellow as Witch Point and its people come to life.

9

I didn't go to school today. When Mae came down for breakfast, she took one look at the dark circles under my eyes and pronounced me ill. I was glad to go along with her. I've spent most of the day sitting around in my pyjamas, playing with the duck called Elvis and patting Duran Duran the donkey while she crunches carrots. I plink a piano key and wish I'd stuck with my lessons. I crash out a tune anyway. It's dramatic and powerful.

'Sounds like a cat dying.' Mae is putting on a sun visor in the hall. 'Did you take that remedy I made for you?'

'Yes.' I actually did. It was a rosewater something or other. It tasted surprisingly nice.

'Well, you look like you've perked up a bit now you've been given a day off school.'

I immediately act extra ill to a 'harrumph' from her.

'I'm just going out to get some shopping. Do you need anything?'

'Nope.'

'No particular requests?'

'Nope.'

'OK. Well, good chatting.' She leaves a wake of sarcasm rippling behind her.

I go to the kitchen and look for something interesting to eat. Hear a loud miaow from upstairs. I ignore it but it soon turns into a howl and even if I can't quite get on with Mrs Danvers, I would never let her be hurt.

At the top of the stairs is an open hatch I've never noticed before. Mrs Danvers is prowling the perimeter. She scowls at me. She is good at climbing up things but not at climbing down apparently.

'OK. OK. Your slave is coming.' I'm not keen on attics. I don't like dark, enclosed spaces. They give me the heebie-jeebies, but I can't just leave her up there stranded.

There's nothing to be scared of.

I start up the ladder. Mrs Danvers watches me. I know who is top dog in this house and it's a cat.

She disappears as I get to the top. Typical. I put

my head through the opening. While it's not pitch black, it is dark enough to be scary. Something swings right in front of my face and I jolt and have to grab the ladder tighter with sweaty hands.

It's just a light cord. Jumpy, much?

I reach forward to pull it. The attic floods with light. 'Wow!'

'I know. Right?' Mrs Danvers doesn't actually voice these words out loud, but her expression says it all. She looks well pleased with herself and I'm not surprised. This is no ordinary attic.

'I expected a couple of suitcases and a few broken boxes.'

She purr-laughs and I do too.

There are trunks everywhere. A spinning wheel with gold thread on a bobbin. An old Singer sewing machine with a peddle. Boxes upon boxes tied with chiffon scarves or string. Hats of every shape and colour. Fear forgotten, I clamber up to investigate.

The temperature is at sauna level, but there's an oval window I squeak open on its hinges. A vague draught struggles in. Looking down, I can see the flowers we rescued from the conservatory. Mrs Danvers wanders out through the porthole across the roof. I guess she must be able to get down? I'll leave the window open anyway.

Pictures of birds of all sorts – some ink drawings, some oil paintings, all museum-old. A galleon in a bottle. Satin ballet shoes, pale blue and moth-eaten. A ship's wheel, which is heavier than I expected. Stars dangle from the ceiling, made of something silver and flimsy, so they flitter and swirl. Swathes of materials make billowing seas. I sift jewel-coloured buttons through my fingers. A chorus of marionettes dangle from hooks. I find a mirror and wrap taffeta around my head, so I look like a pink palm tree.

'Hello?' Dorcas's head pops up through the hatch before I can rip the taffeta off. School must have finished. 'It's a good look for you.'

'I thought so.'

'No one answered, so I let myself in. I hope you don't mind?'

I don't.

'You missed precisely nothing at school.'

I'm glad. I wouldn't like to have missed anything important.

'Yowzers. This place is awesome to the maximum.'

'I know. I only just found it, but it's unbelievable, isn't it?'

Dorcas picks up the ship's wheel and steers it, proving she is stronger than me, then grabs a gold-and-silver turban and puts it on. 'A real collection of curios. Your family are way cool.'

My chest bursts with pride.

Dorcas scoots about, gasping at everything. She kneels down, opens a big trunk full of clothes and starts rummaging through.

Dad said some of my mum's things are stored in this house. I go back to the cold smoothness of the multi-coloured buttons, let them giggle and jingle through my fingers into the jar.

She finds a pair of frilly bathers and shakes them at me. 'Just the thing for our current weather.'

'Have you been to the waterfall the others have been talking about?'

Dorcas looks at me through an iridescent purple sari. 'Yes. The Seven Sisters and the Falls of Snow. Beautiful. We should definitely go. You'd love it.'

'I have been there before. When I was a baby. There's a photo of me and my mum…'

'It would be so lovely and cool there right now. Wild swimming is the absolute best. I went in a lake in Cardiff once and a seriously Baltic one in Snowdonia in the snow. The waterfall would be perfect in this sweltering heat. Sure you don't want to change your mind and put these on?' She shakes the bathers at me again.

'No chance.'

She's having so much fun going through the trunk I decide to brave one myself. I find a donkey's head on the top. It's made of felt and the ears used to have wires to hold them up, but the material has slipped so the ears flop forward and cover the eye holes.

Inside, there are wands painted gold, part of a cardboard wall, and an elaborate moon on a stick. I know what this is. It's the costumes for *A Midsummer Night's Dream*. The production where my dad saw my mum and fell in love with her. I handle each one with care, laying them down gently next to another. Puck. Oberon. A lion's head, that I guess must be one of the players'.

It's there, inside a cotton cover-all. The costume I've seen photos of my mother in. Hermia's dress. It's so beautiful. A shimmering moss-green with leaves around the neckline and a brocade skirt. Tiny gold threads run through the material and it has silver spiderwebs embroidered all over it. I've heard so many stories about it. It doesn't feel real to hold it and know she once wore it. I feel a tear roll down my nose and plop on to the bodice. Then another. I have to sit back from the material or I'll spoil it.

'Are you OK?' Dorcas kneels in front of me. She has an eye patch and a toy seagull clipped to her shoulder.

'It's my mother's. It was my mum's.' I rub my tears away with my palms, but they just keep on flowing. 'They used to put on plays in the garden. This was one of her costumes.'

'That's amazing. It's so beautiful.'

Dorcas is the very best friend I will ever have.

'I don't know why I'm crying. It was so long ago that she died that I can't even really remember her.' I'm trying to stop the tears, but it's no good. 'I think I'm crying for the … I don't know, I think it's the space she left behind. Her absence. Does that make sense?'

I rub more roughly at the tears.

'Of course, it does.' Dorcas moves closer and

puts her arm around my shoulders. 'And don't stop crying. It's a moment of joy and sadness and it deserves tears. That's what my nan always said to me when I was upset.'

I cry hard then. Really, properly cry for everything that isn't. Soon, the tears start to subside, as if I've cried so hard and so fast, they've run out.

'Better?'

'Much.'

'Tears carry excess stress hormones out of your body, it's a well-known fact.'

We both burst out laughing. Our friendship has moved into something new, something more honest and real. It's never happened to me before, but I can feel the shift so clearly and with my whole heart. I can talk to her about anything. I know it.

I ask, 'Who do you think The Witch is?'

'That's so peculiar. I was just wondering the same thing.'

'It could be anyone, couldn't it?'

'I suppose so but, let's look at the facts. It has to be someone who has knowledge of people's histories.'

I nod eagerly because this rules out any chance that I've been sleep-writing.

'But it could be someone who listens to other people's conversations, or knows someone who has lived here a long time and knows everything about everyone in Witch Point. What do you think?' She holds various masks in front of her face. Some of them are sinister, some garishly comic.

'I don't want to point a finger in the wrong direction.'

'Nor me. But it's fun discussing it, isn't it? Perhaps we could be detectives like Sherlock and Watson, or Wells and Wong. Let's try.' She holds up a moveable jaw, and moves it out of time with her words. 'What are the possibilities?'

I actually don't think it's much fun, but I trust her. 'Well. All the letters are written in green ink. Perhaps that's a clue?' I can hear the hope in my voice. I know for a fact that I don't own any pens with green ink. I would have liked one but not now. 'Most of the pens on reception are green.'

'It's worth bearing in mind.' She prances in front of the mirror in a hooped skirt. 'Any other clues?'

'Well, it's probably really stupid and it's just a thought, but do you think Gwyneth could be stirring up all this talk of The Witch to get publicity for her play?'

Dorcas stops dead still. 'Genius. You absolute legend. I bet that's it.'

'Do you think? I mean, I just thought it was a silly idea at first but...' I think about it. Gwyneth is so ambitious. 'It's a possibility.'

I don't like to cast aspersions on anyone. It feels wrong. Like bullying.

'I think we must keep a close eye on her. She is definitely our lead suspect.' Dorcas regretfully puts the costumes back into the trunk. 'I need to go home now. I have chores to do.'

'I'll help you.' I try to stand up, but have to sit down again straight away because I feel woozy. Dorcas rushes over.

'Whoa. Wilde. Are you OK?'

'Yes. I'm fine. It's the heat. I'm OK, honestly.' She helps me to stand. The dizziness is lack of sleep and the heat, I'm certain. 'Dorcas. Can I tell you something?'

'Of course, anything. I'll take it to the grave.'

I believe her. 'I've been sleepwalking. At least I

think I have. I keep waking up in strange places. On the roof. And even weirder, on top of Witch Point windmill. I don't know what's happening to me or what's causing it, but it's really scary and I'm worried I'm going to hurt myself.'

Dorcas looks stunned. 'Wow. You are lucky to be alive.'

'I know.'

She mulls it over. 'I think you're sleepwalking because of the heat. I've definitely read something about that somewhere.'

'How do I stop myself from doing it?' I battle the crack in my voice. 'I haven't slept properly in days.'

'I don't really know but I can stay over if you like? Tomorrow night? I can ask my mam and then I can watch you while you sleep and, if you try to get out of bed, I can stop you.'

'You'd stay awake all night?'

'I'd do my utmost best.'

'Thank you.'

'And tomorrow, in school, let's keep an eye on Suspect One, Fox-Rutherford, first name Gwyneth, and also on the reception desk to see if there are any green pen stealers.'

'It's a plan.'

'Partners in crime. Solving, I mean.'

We shake on it and the world smiles in new colours. I have a real, proper, totally decent friend and I don't have to be afraid.

10

I've hardly slept, and I am way too tired for stupid school. I left my tie hanging over the chair in my bedroom. Mr Ricketts asks where it is and makes sure I know I can't get away with things just because I am the new girl. Mortifying.

We are on our way to Page to Stage. Dorcas is doing a superb impression of Gwyneth and Jemima is doing a vocal warm-up.

'It's a thing I learned from an opera singer. All you have to do is this, three times, and you are as warmed up as it is humanly possible to be.' Jemima makes a noise which goes from a belly-deep nightmare note, to a high-pitched untuned organ, then slides her voice back down again. She does it a second time and I move away. Ivy rolls her eyes at me sneakily. There is dissension in the ranks.

We are in the hall today. It's first lesson so the floors are pretty clean. Gwyneth is parading about, giving us a pep talk. I zone out and watch a group of Year Threes troop past on their way to yet another trip. I wonder what it would be like if I stuck it out here and went up to Witch Point High. Of course, I'm going back to my yellow flat by the sea with my dad, so I won't be, but today I can imagine myself having a really good time and almost wish I was staying.

'The witch called Winter had a sixth sense.'

'Lewis hasn't got a first sense, Miss.'

Raucous laughter and a dead arm for Branwen from Lewis.

'The witch could talk to animals and...'

'Aww, I wish I could talk to animals. That's so cute.' Holly is animal mad. She even has animal badges on her bag.

'Less cute, perhaps, she could trap the spirits of the dead in this world.' Everyone listens intently. 'She trapped the seven sisters in the rivers, so that they would fall from the waterfall to their perpetual deaths forever. Imagine that? Always falling and hitting the ground over and over.'

My stomach is bouncing like a kid on a trampoline. This story is horrible. Why are legends and stories for children always so grim?

Mr Ricketts appears outside the hall and raps the glass to get Gwyneth's attention.

'On with rehearsal, my trusty troupe of troupers.' She leaves with a flourish and we move into our groups.

Holly opens her animal-badged bag and screams. It's another curse.

'No!' Susan Stevens squeals. She looks like she's been crying all night.

'Read it.' Rachel Howells pushes her way into their group.

'She don't have to read it if she don't want to.' Lewis sticks up for everyone. I really like him.

'It's fine. I'll read it. I have nothing to hide.' Holly opens the letter and reads it to us. It's very brave and I admire her for it.

'Dear Holly. A curse for you. We all know you think you are perfect and your sister and friends are perfect too. But do they all know about your nose, Holly? I curse it to grow again until it's as long as an elephant's trunk. Yours faithfully, THE WITCH.'

Ivy's mouth almost hits the floor. Jemima smiles brightly. I don't know what to say. Poor Holly. She stands her ground.

'To be honest, yes, I had my nose altered.'

Ivy rushes towards her.

'No, it's fine, Ivy. I was born with my nose out of shape so the doctor fixed it. It was stopping me breathing properly. None of us is perfect. At least I don't go around being nasty to people.'

She doesn't address anyone by name but almost everyone turns to look at Jemima.

'I've got one too.' Branwen takes it out of her bag shakily.

'Read it then.' Holly scrumples hers in her fist.

'She don't have to read it if she don't…'

'Oh, shut up, Lewis.'

'Dear Branwen…'

I feel sorry for her. She clearly doesn't want to read it. I'm too shy to say anything to help her, which makes me feel really awful.

She clears her throat. 'Dear Branwen. A curse for you. Everyone knows you think you are so clever, but does everyone know you cheated on your exams in October? I don't think so. I curse you to be as stupid as you really are. THE WITCH.'

Branwen tries to think of something brave to say, but before she can there's another gasp as

Thomas finds a letter. He opens it, ready to read, and then closes it, his face drained of blood as if he's been desiccated by a vampire.

'Looks like The Witch is pretty active today. Anyone else?' Jemima smirks.

We all rummage in our bags. Lewis holds one up. His first one had sick all over it so The Witch must have sent another. He unfolds it.

'Read it, Lewis. Oh no, you can't, can you?'

That's not fair. He doesn't deserve that.

'I'll read it for him.' I go and stand next to him. 'If he wants it to be read, that is.'

'I don't have nothing to be 'shamed of.' He does his best to look dignified and I despise the person doing these horrible curses with every bone in my body.

'Dear Lewis.' Everyone is looking at me, which I absolutely hate, but I have to do this. 'You think you are funny, but do you know that everyone is laughing at you rather than with you? You are a fool. I curse you to be laughed at for the rest of your life. THE WITCH.'

Lewis is thoroughly deflated.

'I think you are funny, Lewis. Really, I do. In a really good way,' I say, giving him the note back gently then I wish I'd ripped it up and stamped it into the ground hard.

'I have one.' Dorcas. Oh no. Not Dorcas. My heart is breaking. I don't want her to read it.

'Read it.' Jemima hasn't had one yet, but she seems eager to get everyone else to read theirs. Dorcas pretends to be brave, but I know her better than that now.

'Dear Dorcas. You think you are so interesting with all your facts but let me give you a fact. Everyone knows why you had to…'

'No.' I snatch the note out of her hand and hold it tightly. 'That's enough. Whoever is writing these just wants to cause hurt. To turn us against each other. They are trying to humiliate us.'

'Well, not all of us.' Jemima challenges loudly. 'Have you had a note yet, Wilde?'

The scorch of the sun hammers at the windows. My collar is extra constricting even without my tie. The floor beneath me tips and slides. 'What are you implying?'

'Implying. That's a good word, isn't it, everyone?' Jemima addresses the ogling crowd. 'You are very good with words, aren't you?'

Eyes all over me. I am accused.

'What's going on here?

Gwyneth practically shoves me out of the way in her need to be in the spotlight. 'Are we improvising the execution scene? How marvellous.'

She catches sight of the notes, still in people's hands, and smiles. It's her and her idiotic play, I know it is. All publicity is good publicity. I glance at Dorcas, who is still reeling from her note. I'm going to get Gwyneth and expose her as The Witch. I'm going to…

A call over the tannoy interrupts my thoughts. 'Can Lewis Jones please come to reception? His mam is here with his sun hat.'

None of the usual shrieks of laughter and jeers as he shuffles out.

'A team-building game, I think, and then we rehearse!'

We play pointless games and are then given scenes to improvise.

I overhear Jemima trying to persuade Gwyneth into giving her a bigger part. Gwyneth is adamant that no part is a small part, so Jemima strops out of the room.

The day is stifling and filled with misery. Dorcas is uncharacteristically quiet. She doesn't meet my eye for more than a second. At lunchtime, she goes to a bench at the far side of the yard. I sit next to her.

'Let's set a trap.' I've been thinking about it all morning. 'Let's spread a rumour. Say that we know who it is and that we are going to tell. Then we'll leave the classroom together and The Witch will come running after us and beg for forgiveness. What do you think?'

'It's worth a shot.' She keeps her eyes on the middle distance, looking at the windmill, lilac-blue stone against the dazzling hill. 'My note. It said that I had to…'

'Whoever is writing these notes is an uneducated idiot,' I say over her.

I don't need to know what her note says. There was a space between us, but it closes in this silence and takes us back to where we were. Right next to each other.

'How do we start the rumour?'

'Jemima.' We say it at the same time.

'I'm on it.' I hug Dorcas hard then leave.

Jemima is in the lunch queue. I slide my tray up next to hers. 'Don't tell anyone.' I furtively pretend to check for eavesdroppers. 'I know who The Witch is.'

'Like hell you do.' She pushes my tray back with hers so that they aren't touching. I persevere.

'I do. And me and Dorcas are going to report them this afternoon.' Putting a juice on my tray, I saunter off, knowing that she is watching me leave. That should do it. Glancing back, I see she is already gossiping with Holly and Ivy. I give it about fifteen minutes before the whole population of Witch Point Primary knows.

When afternoon rehearsals begin, just before Gwyneth gives notes, I stand up, interrupting her.

'Miss, me and Dorcas have a very important message we have to deliver to Mr Ricketts.'

You can hear a pin drop.

'Does it have to be now?'

'I'm afraid it does.' Dorcas stands too.

'Then be quick about it.'

We leave the room and feel the weight of expectation coming with us.

Out of sight of the hall, we hide around a corner. We can see the others begin to rehearse. 'Any minute now.'

Gwyneth walks towards the hall exit and we both hold our breath, but she turns and starts talking to Jemima.

'What are you two doing here?' We jump almost out of our skeletons. It's the receptionist with his Witch Point folder.

'Just taking a message, Sir.' Dorcas is better at spontaneous lying than I am.

'Have you delivered it?'

'Yes.'

'Then back you go. Chop chop.'

We go back with our tails between our legs, to rehearse and squabble and slander with the rest of them.

At end of day I go straight home. Everyone has been in strange moods today. There have been random outbursts of crying, snide remarks, sniping. I scuff my school shoes on the path a bit. I need to get out of this horrible play.

What will my note say when it arrives? I dread to think.

I get into Mae's hammock to chill. As I climb in, I'm surprised to find my Shakespeare book there already. I put it on the grass. I don't mind Mae reading it, but I wish she'd asked first. I won't have a go at her though. Why shouldn't she read my book? I'm being an idiot. Getting my balance, I lie back and let the leaf shade dapple me in happiness.

Restless, I reach for *The Collected Works*, and topple out to the ground. The grass is parched but pungently sweet. I feel the familiar cover of the book and open its warm vanilla-perfumed pages. My mum has doodled pictures in the margins. I don't know what they are, but they fascinate me. Swirls and birds, stars and flowers. Some of the doodles are a little bit odd. A girl surrounded by people with their backs turned to her. What looks like a round cage with teeth? I don't know why she would draw these things, but I really wish I did.

I try to let the images speak to me beneath the shade of the trees. There's something there hidden in those pictures. I feel as if I should know what it is.

11

'It looks splendid.'

We stand back and look at our work. We've spent all weekend on it. The treehouse has had a new lick of whitewash on the inside to brighten it up and we've hooked battery-powered fairy lights at the windows which we'll turn on after dark. We've strewn colourful cushions around, and I've brought some of my bits and pieces from my room: the seagull skull, which Dorcas thinks is fascinating; my Shakespeare works, so I can continue to mull over the drawings. I've strung a few feathers I've collected up at the window, where they spin.

'Come on.' Dorcas has whitewash freckles.

We go outside and admire the multi-coloured ribbons rippling from the branches like a rainbow waterfall. 'Good work.'

We have a right to be chuffed, it is mesmerising.

We go back in and flop down on the cushions. I go for turquoise and Dorcas egg-yolk yellow.

'We should give it a name.' I pass Dorcas a paintbrush. 'Then we can make a sign to put up outside.'

'Good idea. What about calling it the most fantabulous treehouse in the world?' We both look at the piece of wood and laugh. 'It's not going to fit, is it?'

'The Snug?' I've always liked that word.

'Or The Wilde Place?'

I like that and it's kind of Dorcas to suggest it, but I want it to be both of ours. 'What about WildeDorcas?'

'It doesn't really trip off the tongue.'

'OK. The Crow's Nest?'

'Ooh. I like that. Like on a ship, Captain Wilde.'

'Correct, Captain Dorcas.' I salute. 'We can bring the ship's wheel down from the attic and the telescope from the porch to help us look out for pirates.'

'Good idea, but you can't really have two captains.'

'It's our treehouse. We can do what we like.' We salute each other in solidarity.

'Well, isn't this sweet.'

I jump and knock a bottle of red paint over. It splats the yellow cushion like blood.

Jemima stands in the doorway, backed by Holly and Ivy. 'A lovely little playhouse for two lovely little friends.'

'What do you want, Jemima?'

'Oh, I don't know. Nothing in particular. We thought we'd come and have a chat with you. Didn't we, girls?' She struts into the treehouse, sneering. Ivy and Holly stay in the doorway. 'So, what actually is this place?'

'It's a treehouse. What does it look like?' Dorcas is scraping red off the cushion and her leg.

'Thank you, Dorc-ass, for that brilliant explanation, but I meant what are you doing up here together?' Jemima pronounces 'Dorcas' emphasising the syllables separately. I can see that it really riles Dorcas.

'Look. You aren't invited here,' I shout. 'You are trespassing on my property and if you don't leave, I will call the police and have you arrested.' This is silly. There aren't any police in Witch Point. I fold in on myself like an envelope.

'Ooh. I'm scared.' Jemima inspects the

treehouse, sniffing her disgust at everything. 'What's this?'

She picks up my seagull skull as if it is the filthiest specimen she has ever had the misfortune to come across, as if we are forcing her to handle it.

I bristle. 'Put that down.'

It's one of my favourite possessions. I'm certain that's weird, but it's also true.

'Eww. Why have you got a dead bird in here?'

'Everything dies eventually.' It comes out like a threat.

'Oh no. I'm even more scared now.' She doesn't look scared. She looks thrilled. 'Are you, I don't know, I don't mean to pry, but are you using this place to cast spells? Is there a cauldron here somewhere?'

That horrible spiteful nasty sow. The tree creaks, sending out warning signals through its roots. Danger, danger. The birds pick up the call and caw and cwarak. I try to laugh it off but I'm not convincing. 'Don't be so childish.'

'I'm not the one playing in a treehouse, little girl.'

Ivy's phone pings, closely followed by Holly's. 'We have to go home. It's teatime.'

Jemima is on a mission to cause trouble. 'Go on

then. Run along. I think I'll hang out here a bit longer.'

They leave with apologetic expressions to me and Dorcas. They aren't so bad. Nowhere near as bad as Jemima. Do they even like her very much? It makes me feel sad for her. I know what it's like to struggle to find a friend. Surprising myself, I say, 'You can stay if you want to. We are just painting a sign for the door.'

She contorts her face. We wait for a blistering insult, but she pulls up a scarlet cushion and sits on it. Dorcas has to pick her jaw up off the floor. I want to tread carefully.

'You don't have to paint, but you can if you like?' I pass Jemima a paint brush. 'We are trying to make the place as colourful as possible so use as many as you want. We did those earlier.'

Our paintings look clumsy, but this is my space, I want it to be cheerful and they are anything but dull. 'Yours can go there. Paint anything you like.'

Jemima holds the paintbrush as if it might sting her. I put a piece of paper down in front of her. Dorcas looks at me as if I have gone completely mad, but puts the jar of water in front of Jemima and carries on painting our sign. She even whistles. I love her for it.

'I … I don't know what to paint.' Jemima holds the brush limply.

'I've done some paintings of places around the world and some flowers too. They're the easiest.' I point to the one I did earlier. 'I mean, mine is just a collection of blue dots, like Impressionism. Any way you want. The brighter the better.'

I pretend to be absorbed in stringing beads, even though the tree doesn't need another garland. Dorcas carries on whistling. Jemima carries on staring at the blank paper.

Through the window I can see a jackdaw hopping along the branch. It is joined by another, and then another. I carry on stringing beads and Dorcas keeps whistling, but you can hear that her lips are getting dry and it's getting harder for her to produce any sound.

I start singing. Just like that.

'Summertime and the living is easy. Fish are jumping…'

I clear my throat. We've been learning this song in school with Mr Ricketts at registration, so we all know it. 'Fish are jumping, and the cotton is high.'

'Your daddy's rich and your momma's good looking.' Dorcas joins in and I smile sing.

'So, hush little baby, don't you cry.' We take a breath to carry on, but we don't need to.

'One of these mornings...' Jemima's voice is rich as toffee. Deep and soulful. 'You're gonna rise up singing. Then you'll spread your little wings and take to the sky.'

She starts to paint as she sings. Big strokes of orange, before twizzling her brush in the water and painting spirals of yellow buttercup. It's joyful, the three of us here like this.

We join in with her, but we are only the backing singers to a star. More birds gather on the tree outside. I think they are charmed by the beauty of her voice. Her phone beeps sharply and she stops.

'Sorry, losers. Something better has come up...' She scribbles out her painting and tosses the brush, so it spatters the floor.

'We were just trying to be nice.'

'I don't need your *nice*.' She stands up and glowers at us as if we have conned her into something. 'I don't need you to feel sorry for me.'

'We didn't.' I stand up too and the beads come

loose from their string and scatter to the corners. 'We just thought you might like to be friends.'

'Hah! With you?' So scornful. 'Not likely. And for your information, I know it's you.' Jemima jabs her finger at me. 'You pretend you are just silly little kids with your silly little treehouse, and your silly little paintings and your silly little... What even is this?'

She picks up the skull again and throws it down. It splinters along the lower jaw. It's like I feel the break in my own bones.

'No!' I can't move I'm so shocked. Dorcas runs to pick it up.

'You are the one writing the curses. My mother says the curse has come back stronger than ever since you've been here. Your mother was evil and so are you.'

The birds jabber outside.

'When I catch you, and I will catch you, I am going to make sure that you suffer.'

I can't move. I can't speak. Her accusations are ringing in my ears, but I can't defend myself.

Dorcas walks towards her and Jemima backs away, but keeps stabbing her finger at me like a dagger.

'Witch.' Stab. Stab. 'Put a spell on me, go on. Just like your mother did. Put spells on everyone. I know. My mother told me. She was a wicked witch and one day her spells went wrong and she cursed herself and died.'

My heartbeat has stopped. Dorcas is crying. How dare Jemima talk about my mother like that? I could kill. I could kill.

I raise my finger and point at her with every ounce of power I can summon. 'I curse you to die.'

The words are savage, bitter. They shock me. The birds screech and agitate the branches.

Jemima is going to die. Right here. I will have murdered someone.

She claws at her throat with both hands and panic flashes in her eyes.

No. No. I don't want her to die. Please. No.

'Pathetic.' Jemima takes her hands away from her throat and sneers at me. 'Did you really think that would work? Just saying: "I curse you".'

She does an impression of me in a weaselly, babyish voice.

'You'll have to try harder than that, hag breath, because I am pretty powerful myself, you know.' She is wild with anger, loud above the screech of the birds. 'I'm going to catch you and your servant.' She pushes Dorcas into the wall. 'And when I catch you, I'm going to make sure everyone knows what a horrible, poisonous witch you are.'

She grabs hold of my Shakespeare book and throws it full force out the window. I charge after it. Watch it spilt apart and take wing, a flock of birds. My mum's book.

I start to shake all over as pages flock to the grass.

Jemima leaves, a triumphant expression on her face. Dorcas is straight out after her.

I go outside. There are pages scattered across the garden. The cover has landed near the brook. The birds circle the ladder as I climb down on legs of blancmange.

I'm OK. Go away now.

I can vaguely hear Dorcas and Jemima arguing in the road but I just need to get the pages back so I don't pay them much attention. I grab one before Duran Duran starts munching on it. Unhook some from the thorns of the roses. Rescue them from the wild flowerbeds. One is a little damaged from the fountain.

My mum's drawings. I put them back in order and hold them close to my heart in a hug.

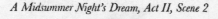

TITANIA

...The clamorous owl that nightly hoots and wonders
At our quaint spirits. Sing me now asleep;
Then to your offices and let me rest.

The Fairies sing
I
You spotted snakes with double tongue,
Thorny hedgehogs, be not seen;
Newts and blind-worms, do no wrong,
Come not near our fairy queen.
Chorus
Philomel, with melody
Sing in our sweet lullaby;
Lulla, lulla, lullaby, lulla, lulla, lullaby:
Never harm,
Nor spell nor charm,
Come our lovely lady nigh;
So, good night, with lullaby.
II
Weaving spiders, come not here;
Hence, you long-legg'd spinners, hence!
Beetles black, approach not near;
Worm nor snail, do no offence.
Chorus
Philomel, with melody, &c

FAIRY

Hence, away! now all is well:
One aloof stand sentinel.

12

For once I leave quickly for school. Mae and Jules are arguing in the kitchen. The plants are dying, even though they have been moved into the shade. Mae is taking it out on Jules. Her business depends on the flowers. She's even put the wi-fi on to sort out her orders. I quickly use my phone to check for messages from Dad. I send him one back to let him know I'm OK and that I miss him. I don't tell him that I love him because he'll think that something's wrong. I give the phone back to Mae without arguing. Jules is trying to calm her down but, like everyone else in this heat, she is burnt at the edges with anger.

I slept well for the first time in forever because of absolute exhaustion, I think. I might have walked somewhere in my sleep and not remembered it, but there are no new scratches or bruises on me, and my pyjamas have no dirty patches or tears.

'Bye,' I yell from the hallway. I'd rather skip breakfast than talk about how Mae's handmade soaps are sweating or how claggy her homemade toothpastes are getting. I am not responsible for everything and I have bigger fish to fry.

When I get to school, the yard is strangely silent. I'm ready for a run-in with Jemima and almost disappointed not to get it over with. Some of my class are sitting in the shade but most of them must have already gone inside.

'Wilde. Wait up.'

It's Lewis. His shirt is grubby and his shoes are worse for wear. I feel sad for him. He's such a nice boy.

'Hi, Lewis. How's it going?'

'Good, ta. I've been swimming this morning. Wanted to stay there all day but they'd send me home from school tomorrow if they found out I'd bunked off today and I don't want to lose my part in the play.'

'Because of the axe?'

'Exactly.'

I'm so jealous of the swimming.

'Still, at least if I got sent home I could go swimming again.'

Where there's Lewis, there's logic.

'Did you go to the waterfall?'

'Yup. It's freezing. Makes you get ice-cream head, you know?'

I do know. I got it when I went surfing off Caswell Bay. It's not much fun in reality but in this heat it seems like a glorious memory. 'I haven't been there yet.'

'Seriously. You have to go. It's stupendous.'

We move as slowly as we can to the hall for rehearsals. If we were walking backwards, we'd probably get there faster. Lewis sees the axe prop and practically leaps across the room to try it out on one of the boys' arms.

The class is thin on the ground. Dorcas is here already, holding a cauldron and a big wooden spoon. She puts it down when she sees me and comes straight over.

'Are you OK? I gave Jemima such a mouthful yesterday. I was going to come back, but my mam grabbed me and made me go shopping with her.'

The boy Lewis is pretending to strike with an axe takes his arm away at the last second and Lewis stumbles and brings the blade down with a thud on his own foot. 'Argh!' Though it's only made of wood it must really hurt because his head becomes a beetroot. I want to help him, but Gwyneth comes in and grabs all the attention as per always.

'Focus in, guys. I said, focus in.' She clicks her fingers and we straggle towards her and sit on the floor. She runs through notes for the play. I look around at my classmates. Lewis, whose heart is gold and head is bright red. Dorcas, the best friend I have ever had. Branwen, who I don't know well yet but seems alright. The boy who was being axed, Cai – that's it. Susan, red-eyed as always. Holly. No Ivy. No Jemima. All the others look tired. These curses have really taken it out of us and, I've just realised, have only been aimed at people in this class. I give Gwyneth a dirty look.

Dorcas leans over and whispers to me. 'She is loving every minute of this.'

Gwyneth glares in our direction, then starts. 'Our motivation is to bring a mirror to life. The curses are real. Winter is real. We are all going to die terrible, terrible deaths and it is all Winter's fault. That's what we want to say to our audience. With the amount of energy you lot are putting into your characters, you wouldn't be able to act your way out of a paper bag. We want people to be afraid of the ancient curse. To be unable to sleep at night. To clutch at their hearts as the sun goes down and breathe a sigh of relief when...'

She's interrupted by the receptionist banging on the glass. She tells us to sit and contemplate our acting. We all start chatting as soon as she's gone. Dorcas leans in close.

'Do you still think it's her?'

I nod. It's the only explanation. We watch her like hawks as she chats to the receptionist, who is flicking through his Witch Point folder.

'How does she know so much about us?'

'Well, he has access to all our records, and they look pretty buddy, buddy to me.'

'You're right.'

As we watch, Jemima appears and talks to them. She comes into the classroom. She sits quietly next to Holly. I don't know where Ivy is. Jemima seems curiously subdued. I expected her to be gloating and proud. I look around my classmates. Everyone looks tired and miserable. What's happened to us?

Gwyneth comes back in, wailing as if in agony. Whatever this is, it's going to be bad.

'I have a terrible announcement.' She sits heavily and lets us wait, enjoying the drama. 'Prepare yourselves for grave news.'

We take a collective breath in.

'Ivy has been taken ill.'

Holly fidgets.

'She is not well enough to perform in the play. As we are so close to performance, we will have to make rash casting decisions.'

I see Jemima sit up straight, a hopeful expression on her face.

'I will now play the role of Winter myself.' Gwyneth plays the martyr, pretending she's doing it for us and not for herself.

Silence.

'What's wrong with Ivy, Miss?' Lewis is so kind about everyone. He is genuinely concerned.

'She has some kind of inexplicable bug. Sickness. Diarrhoea.'

We all squirm. No one wants other kids to know that they have diarrhoea.

'I think the curse may be upon her.'

No.

'I'm afraid I shall have to take over the role of Winter!'

Double no.

My hand flies up. 'Miss, Jemima could play the part.'

Whatever I think of Jemima, that's what should happen. I watch Gwyneth. She acts as if she is considering this casting, scratches her chin, folds her arms, muses. She is not a good actor at all.

'No, no. I fear it would be too much to put upon her.'

'It wouldn't, Miss. I could do it,' Jemima begs.

'No, no. I think it's best if I take on the burden.' Gwyneth adopts a pseudo-brave expression and I loathe her. 'It will no doubt bring in a crowd. I have quite the following on social media. I shall need to spend some time learning the lines, so you must all go to your various groups and lead yourselves today. We shall fit it all together this afternoon. Fear not, I will not let you down. Once a professional, always a star!'

She flounces outside.

'What's really wrong with Ivy?' Cai asks Holly. We all listen in, some of us pretending not to.

'I don't know. She's like vomming everywhere. I took her curse note out of the bin at home and it said that being the lead had gone to her head and sickness would bring her back down to earth. I think the fear has gotten to her.'

I take Dorcas to the opposite wall. 'Convinced it's Gwyneth yet?'

She gives a low whistle.

'We are going to catch her. I'm not sure how yet, but we are.'

'It's not fair that she's going to play the lead role. We'll be a laughing stock.'

I pretend to string up a noose in my role as hangman and watch Gwyneth take an overly dramatic bow to an invisible audience. She planned this all along. I just know it.

Lots of the class are whispering. We are all under suspicion, but no one is pointing at Gwyneth. Branwen and Susan are pointing at me. They turn away when I glare in their direction. Rachel and Manon point at Jemima then shake their heads and assess me too. Lewis is pointing at a splatter of sick on his trousers. No one is talking about the real culprit, who is starting to sign imaginary autographs for imaginary fans.

Birds pattern the sky beyond her, but I will them away. I'm going to catch this woman myself and when I do there'll be hell to pay.

13

It's getting dark finally. I really need to sleep, but it's so weird having Dorcas here staring at me.

'Sniff this.' She shoves a bunch of lavender in my face. A sprig goes up my nose.

'Ow, you idiot.'

'It's meant to be therapeutic.'

'Not when you stab me up my nostril, it isn't.'

'Sorry.' She yawns. This isn't going to work if she falls asleep too. Seeing my worry, she slaps her cheeks to rouse herself. Poor Dorcas. She hasn't been sleeping well either. 'I'm here. Present. On watch. I. Will.' *Slap.* 'Not.' *Slap.* 'Fall.' *Slap.* 'Asleep.' *Slap, slap.*

'Good.'

'You, however, can feel free to sleep at any time now.' She is sitting in a chair right next to me. 'Seriously. Any time you like.'

'Perhaps if you move away a bit.'

'Oh yeah. Of course.' She moves the chair to the other side of the room and stares at me.

This is such a ridiculous plan, but Dorcas will guide me back to the bed if I start to sleepwalk. We know it's dangerous to wake up someone who is sleepwalking, but I reckon it's more dangerous to let them climb on a roof, so I'll take my chances.

'Wilde, you have to actually close your eyes to go to sleep. Count sheep or something. I don't know. Put a pillow over your head.'

'It's too hot. I'd die of asphyxiation.'

'Good word.'

'Thank you.'

'Now stop saying words and…'

'I know. I know. I'm trying.'

'Try harder.'

I close my eyes and Gwyneth appears immediately. She jigs about in a Halloween witch's costume then puts a pumpkin on her head as a helmet and rides off on a broomstick with a banner advertising the show trailing behind her. I'm sure it's her writing the curses. I'm sure that we can catch her.

'Stop thinking about wreaking revenge on Gwyneth and go to sleep.'

Dorcas knows me better than almost anyone else already.

I open my eyes enough to see Dorcas. She's messaging someone on her phone. I wonder who it is?

Could it be Dorcas writing the curses? No. I tell myself off. I turn away.

I'll count sheep. One, two, three. I try to make them turn uphill, but they won't. Stubborn sheep. The owls land and scratch the roof above with their talons. I imagine Mrs Danvers licking her lips as she looks at them. I'll count birds instead. I've always liked them. Nice friendly birds. I think of them gathering, following me, swooping down to peck at people. Not helping me sleep at all.

I sit up.

'I can't talk to you right now.' Dorcas puts her palm towards me and carries on messaging. I grab the water spray I've brought up and soak my sheets. Dorcas's lit-up face rolls its eyes then pointedly ignores me. I lie back down.

The water is soothing. I think of swimming. The wriggles of light on the yellow walls of my room in our flat by the sea. Dad and me out on a boat. The waves gently rocking us, just me and him. Magical glints of white against lifts of azure blue. It's just us two and the ocean. Just us and the dreaming, drifting, endless rolling blues.

'Argh!' I fall. I wake with a bump. It takes me a second to get my bearings.

It's fine. It's good. I'm in my room. I'm on the floor by the witch window, but I'm inside. It's all good. It's dark. The lamp is on the floor and there's a strange noise coming from the other side of the room. Dorcas.

I reach for the lamp and turn it on. 'Dorcas?'

She's cowering on the far side of the room.

'Dorcas. What is it?'

'There are no facts to support this. There have been rumours, sightings even, but there's no scientific evidence.'

I go towards her and she backs away, still muttering incoherently about there being no facts.

'Dorcas, what is it?'

'Somnambulism. Sleepwalking. Yes. But this. No. No facts. No facts to support.'

She's like an android having a meltdown. 'Dorcas, you're scaring me.'

Mae's voice yells up the stairs. 'Wilde?'

Oh, for goodness sake. 'Dorcas. It's Mae. I'm just going to head her off. I'll be back. Just calm down. Calm down!' I dash out.

Mae stands at the bottom of the narrow stairs, rumpled in her nightshirt and clearly cross as well as concerned. 'What's the matter?'

'Sorry, Mae. We were just messing about. I was telling Dorcas a ghost story, you know that one about the girl in the green dress, and she got scared and screamed. That's all. I promise we'll go to sleep now.'

'I'll put my earplugs in. Carry on. As you were.'

She goes and I sprint back up the stairs.

Dorcas is still jabbering away to herself.

'It's fine. I told Mae a little lie, but she's fine.'

Jabbering random facts is Dorcas's way of calming down. I let her do it for a bit, but curiosity and irritation overwhelm me.

'What are you talking about? Dorcas, tell me.'

I take the glass of water from the side of the bed. I can't bring myself to throw it in her face, like I've seen people do on films, so I flick some of it at her with my fingers. On the third flick her eyes focus on me.

'Wilde.' She studies me so strangely.

'Dorcas.' I wait. I have no idea what is coming. What if she is the one writing the curses and is about to confess? I'll forgive her. She's my friend. If she did it there's a good reason.

'I don't even know how to say this.' Her voice wavers an entire musical scale.

'Just spit it out, Dorcas. Whatever it is. We'll deal with it, OK?'

'Not this.'

'Just tell me.'

She's not even looking at me now. I feel so sorry for her. This is horrific. She is going to confess to being The Witch.

'Wilde. You were...' She hugs herself for comfort. 'You were flying.'

'What?' I burst out laughing. 'What?' It's the only word I have.

She still doesn't look at me.

It's a joke. A prank. I bet she's filming my reaction. Her phone is clutched in her hand, but it's not on.

'Dorcas. I don't get it. What's the joke?'

'It isn't a joke.' She keeps hugging herself, like her arms are some sort of protection against me.

'Dorcas. Stop it. You're freaking me out.'

'You were flying, Wilde. I was looking at my phone and you were sleeping and then there was this sound, like a whoosh, and you were by the window. In the air by the window. Your feet weren't on the floor. And I screamed and you dropped, but you were flying. You were flying.'

'Don't be ridiculous.'

'You were flying. There is no other explanation for what I saw. You were flying.'

I think of all the places I've woken up. High places.

Ridiculous.

I think of all the things that have happened to me in the past. Weird things. Dreams of flying. Birds. The stories about my mother. I know deep down that I am different. But this?

'Did you film it? This alleged flying?' This is a childish joke. Childish and upsetting.

'I...'

'Well? It's a simple enough question, isn't it?'

'I was too scared.'

Dorcas was scared of me. That hurts, and it shows.

'Shocked, I mean. I was too ... shocked to...' She uses the wall to stagger up. 'It makes no sense.'

'You're right. It doesn't.' My voice is filled with spite, and for once, I don't care. 'Do you think perhaps you fell asleep, Dorcas?' I'm leaning in at her, threatening. 'That you might have been dreaming?'

I want to stop being this person and help her because she looks so petrified, but I can't. I won't have this nonsense hurled at me. I trusted her. I thought she was my friend.

'I wasn't dreaming, Wilde. I wasn't. I kept playing that world-building game on my phone to make sure I stayed awake and … you were in the air. You were. In the air.'

I want to smash things. Shake her so she'll take it back. The witch windows rattle and blow open.

'I'm going, Wilde. I'm sorry.'

I try to calm down. 'You're supposed to be staying here overnight.'

'I forgot I have to do something.'

'In the middle of the night?' My fury fills the room, drawing the night closer.

'I'm sorry.' She keeps her back to the wall as she leaves, as if she thinks I'm going to attack her. I watch her clatter down the stairs and out of sight.

'Dorcas. I'm not going to do anything. Dorcas.' I whisper after her.

I look out, feeling the beckoning swirl of treacle night air. I rush to the window and hold onto the frame hard.

Dorcas runs down the path, looking back at me fearfully as she goes.

It can't be true. It's impossible.

I close the windows, latch them, then examine myself in the mirror. There's nothing different in my reflection.

Dorcas was dreaming. She must have been.

Something shadows the mirror, though there's nothing in the room. The owls scratch the roof. I sit facing straight into the mirror, searching for something that is trying to show itself to me, until dawn bleeds into the room and I have to take on another awful day. This time I'm alone.

14

I am going to the waterfall for a swim and no one is stopping me. Not Dorcas, who probably hates me now as much as I hate her. Not school, because I'm not telling them. Not Mae, because I'm not telling her either.

The bracken crackles and something snickers through it. I put my hands above my eyes to shade them from the bellowing sun. The grass is tinder and there have been lots of wildfires on the hillsides because of the heat. I'm nervous the whole undergrowth will start smoking and catch.

I've brought my *Collected Works of Shakespeare*. I've taped the pages back in and I want to keep it close. It doesn't seem like the brilliant idea it was when I first set out. It's making my bag heavy and I can feel an angry pain building in my temple as it bangs into my spine with every step.

All the other kids will be in school. I can't face

it. I want to have some time alone, in a place my mother loved. I can still see the school not too far away and worry that they'll be able to see me. I'm just being paranoid.

The water in my forever bottle is warm and plasticky. I'm going to get a bamboo bottle soon. The water will still be warm but woody warm has to be better than this hot sick taste. A heron breaks the distant sky. I could be walking through the Jurassic period. Where there's a heron, there's water. The seven sisters were trapped in the rivers forever by Winter.

Something shakes the gorse. I think of adders. No one has died from an adder bite in years. A fact I read in a book Dorcas recommended. I'm not thinking about Dorcas because she is a snake. *Think about facts instead.*

Adder bites are very rare. Shark bites are even rarer. I miss the sea. I miss my dad. I keep wanting to tell him when I speak to him, but I don't because I don't want to upset him. I miss my mum, which surprises me. I feel like I could cry for her again. But I haven't the energy. If I'm going to give in to tears, I'll wait till I'm at the waterfall and cool.

The ground falls away steeply and I hear something which makes my heart sing. The sound of water. There are steep steps cut out of the earth, held by wood and iron bolts.

My mum came here. The witch called Winter came here. I won't think of the play. Or Dorcas. Of course I can't fly. If I could fly, surely I'd just leap into the air now? I jump, to try, and land with a thump.

I start down. I'm here to talk to my mum. It's odd to admit this, even inside my head, but it's the truth. She loved this place and if I ever needed her, I need her now. I need advice.

She was a witch.

Mae told me, when I was six. I remember Mae arguing with my dad afterwards. She said I had to know the truth and he said it was his decision. I wasn't to know. He said she was never to say it again. They think I don't remember because I was very young.

It's as clear as the chime of a bell. I've always pretended to myself that Mae was making crazy accusations. It's easy to dismiss what Mae says. But I've always known deep down she spoke the truth. I've always known my mum was a witch.

The truth runs in my blood. But I don't want to be a witch too.

The water zings through the trees in blinking lights, spangling their leaves in sequins. There's a resting place with a sign about the local wildlife and a mention of the legend. There is an illustration of a comical hag with a green face, pointed boots and boils on her nose. Winter.

That story isn't right. That tug inside again. Like something attached to my belly button. I need to know what the real story is.

Emerald and chattering, the water welcomes me. I slide my bag off gratefully, stretching out and admiring its rippling jade beauty. So, this is it. The Falls of Snow. It glitters a greeting. It's meant to be extremely dangerous in the winter because of ice and the extreme rainfall in Wales. Now, in a drought, it's impossible to see anything but beauty. There's no one else here.

I test the water with my fingers. Cold to the point of burning. So cold I have to take my hands straight out and shake them. So deliciously cold I have to put them straight back in. I have my swimsuit on underneath my shorts. It's a bit small because it's from last year, but it'll do, if I can get up the courage to go in. I've swum in the sea before, but never when I'm alone, Dad is really clear about that. As I've flouted all the rules already, what's one more? The water level looks low.

Checking again to make sure there's no one here, I strip down and negotiate the rocks in bare feet. It's so good to get my shoes off. I sit on a large rock and wriggle my toes into the water first. My feet have welts on them, from wearing daps with no socks, and the water soothes the blisters. My ankles pulse the cold.

Looking up, the water fizzes and pours over the mouth of the waterfall. Droplets catch the sun and become rainbows. The pool it has created in the rocks is mythical. I can see why people make up stories about it. This green cauldron drummed into the earth.

I lower my ankles further into the shallow parts, so I'm up to my shins. My feet look deathly blue beneath the khaki whorls of water and I paddle out over slippery rocks to where the river deepens. The current isn't strong because of the lack of rain, but I'm going to be cautious anyway. It can be very dangerous to go straight into cold water on a hot day. I wade further towards the bowl at the base of the cliff. The others go swimming here so it must be safe enough. Dorcas goes swimming here. Thinking of her makes my heart tingle and my eyes itch. I'm going in.

I push my body forward into the pool. Break the water with my hands and swim out to the centre, gasping for breath, feeling my heart race, treading fast to keep warm. I hold my nose and duck beneath the surface to see if I can open my eyes. I can't. I want to be part of the watery world. To lose myself in this beautiful jewel. I come up for air, the water's song trilling in my ears. Startling reality snaps in. Birds. Heat. The roar of the fall as it snows against the cliff.

I'll give it one more shot. Holding my nose and bracing myself I duck again and let my body float, face downwards. I open my eyes. Close them in panic. Open them again. I can see.

The world is bouncing and vibrant. Green and murky. Yellow lightning flashes. Dusty and powder blue. I push downwards. Teal, the deep green of a rock pool, the lime, slivering weeds.

All those witches dunked and drowned. Did they do that here? All their souls lurking forever, waiting for revenge. The seven sisters perpetually falling to their deaths. Something reaches out through the weeds.

I burst up and out of the water, race to the side, scrabble against the rocks to get out, stand in the bright air. I make sure my feet are out of the water, for fear of something dragging me back under.

Hallucinations again. Brought on by the difference in temperatures. Stupid thing, to swim alone.

I'm going to sit here with my book now and stay out of the water. I'm going to look at the pictures my mum left. I flick through them. Try to understand. I should feel close to her here. That's what I was hoping for. But nothing is any clearer. Maybe she just liked doodling and I'm making too much of this. Maybe I'm searching desperately for some kind of connection. Between the pictures. Between me and her. If she'd wanted to tell me something, why wouldn't she have just written me a letter?

Unless whatever she was trying to tell me *had* to be kept a secret?

I try to piece the images together and come up with nothing but frustration.

Come on, Mum. I need you. I really need you.

An unexpected breeze drifts across my shoulders and I look up at the waterfall. There's something behind it. A figure? No, there's only one way in there and no one has passed me. Unless they went while I was under the water? No, I wasn't there for long enough. I strain my eyes to see through the gaps in the cascade. A ghost? No, I don't believe in ghosts.

You said you didn't believe in curses, but you're having second thoughts about that one.

With relief, I see that it's a bird. A red kite. Stuck there, by the looks of it. What if it can't get out? I need to help it. Perhaps the water is too fast for it to fly through. I can't just leave it there.

At the side of the waterfall, there is a rough path hewn out of the rock. I hadn't planned trying to climb it while I was here alone, because of all the warnings about people falling, but now I have to. I'm going to help that bird.

I keep my back against the slick cliff. Some of the water rebounds off the rocks and sprays up into my face. I move slowly and with care. I don't want to slip into the pool beneath me. Hallucination or not, it was scary.

The others were right, there's a space where you can walk behind the water, a sort of shallow cave. The kite is at the far end. It won't be able to hear me because the water is thunderous, but I still make soft noises, not to alarm it. Kites don't befriend people unless they feed them. It won't come near me. I'm soaked to the skin as the water hollers down. A cathedral of moving white. A million voices of water shout and whistle and sing.

'It's OK. I won't hurt you. I'm going to help you to get out.'

It flies directly at me. I topple and almost fall. The kite breaks through the water wall and is gone, leaving me in this echoing kingdom of sound and light. I laugh until I'm completely out of breath.

It's so wondrous here. I reach out with my hands and play the cascades like harp strings. I watch the world beyond in shimmering pictures. The gorge and the river beyond the water bounce and waltz.

The view changes shape. What's happening? Pictures are appearing in the water. Real pictures. Obscuring the valley beyond. Women dancing. Firelight. A family. A cottage and a girl at the window.

'Your mother could see things, Wilde. In glass. In water.'

Mae used a strange word. Something like crying. Scrying. That was it. The movements in the mirror. The pictures become clearer in front of me. I'm trapped by them. Watching the water morphing to show me image after image. The sunlight filters through, making it like a film screen.

They are starting to make sense, the dancing shadows. They are telling me a story. The story of Winter and what really happened. The pictures from my mother's book all slot together and she is here in my heart and in the story I have to tell.

I watch it all play out in this world of water. I know the real story. I've always known it. And now I'm the one who has to tell it.

15

I've missed lots of rehearsal, but I don't care. All this twaddle Gwyneth has spouted about the legend. It's all wrong. I have to put it right, but I'm worried. They all think I'm weird already, and I just wanted to fit in somewhere for once. Dorcas hasn't spoken to me or even glanced in my direction, and I bet everyone else has noticed. Today is a dress rehearsal. Gwyneth, wearing a preposterous pointed hat, is leading everyone through what the class are now calling 'The Gwyneth Show'.

Tomorrow is the end of term. Tomorrow is the show. The pressure is building in the air and inside my brain.

'Miss, I need the toilet.'

She wafts me away while she tricks the seven sisters into following her into the snow. Tomorrow Lewis will have bits of recycled confetti to shake over them but today he just has an empty sieve which he is wearing over his face like a fencing mask.

I skulk to the girls' toilets to get away from this claptrap. The picture of Winter pleads with me from the wall.

I know. I promised I'd tell your story and I will.

'Wilde. Where are you going?'

The receptionist. He's always wandering around the corridors spying on people. I wonder that he gets any work done at all.

'Toilet, Sir.'

'Do you have permission?'

'Yes.'

'Good, good.' He holds that file again. It's like he doesn't want to let it go. 'You aren't feeling sick, are you? I noticed you've been off school.'

He notices everything. Mae says he comes from a family of gossips.

'I'm fine now.'

'That's good news. It will be a blessing to have a break in this heat, won't it?' He wipes his fingers across his brow and leaves green smudges.

'Sir. You've got green across your head.'

He looks down and his fingertips are covered in green. Taking out a tissue he wipes at them then disappears to spy on someone else presumably. Green fingers. Green ink. *Don't be daft.*

The girls' toilet is a sanctuary. There are no shadows in the mirror to catch my eye. Nothing is reflected but the pink walls, the cool tiles, the empty cubicles. I check for feet underneath the doors. None. In the distance, the bell goes for break. I turn the constant drip of a tap to full and splash my face then use two hands to turn it off properly.

Dorcas comes in. She clearly isn't expecting me.

'Oh.' She stops and realises that she can't really walk back out without saying anything. 'I didn't know you were in here.'

'I'm sorry, I didn't know you owned the toilets.'

'I just…'

'Why are you avoiding me, Dorcas?' I know the answer, but I want her to say it.

'I just…'

'Go on.'

'OK, I will if you let me speak.'

'Oh, I'll let you speak alright, but I tell you what, Dorcas, if it's so difficult, I'll fill in the details. Well, Wilde, the reason I've been avoiding you like the plague is because I accused you of flying the other night and then did a runner, leaving you shocked and bewildered and really, really, REALLY upset.'

'It's just…'

'Is that it? Is that all you can say?'

'I can't process the information. I can't believe what I saw.'

'Oh, yeah. Because you saw me flying, right? Where's the evidence, Dorcas? Or did you just make it up? Because, like you said so many times, there are no facts to support this. And, funnily enough, Dorcas, humans can't fly. There's a fact for you. A well-known fact.'

'I don't tell lies. You know that.'

'I know you told me that. But you could have been lying.'

'If we are going to talk about lying, then why don't you tell me why you're doing it?'

'Flying?'

'No. Writing the curses.'

This is the sharpest slap I've ever received. It takes the breath from my body. I can't make words. I am so hurt. My head is shaking a 'no', but the world is in slow motion and I'm holding the pain in so tight.

'Just tell me why, Wilde? I can help you.'

I am a balloon bursting. 'How dare you? How dare you pretend to be my friend and then turn on me like this? I hate you. I hate you.' I'm grabbing hold of her and snarling in her face. She's fighting back and she's really hurting me, but my anger is stronger and won't be stopped. Suddenly there is someone else there, pulling us apart.

'Stop. Stop.'

It's Susan Stevens.

I back away from Dorcas. I'm out of breath and stunned.

Susan Stevens. How much has she heard?

'I want it to stop now. It's all gone too far.' Susan is crying. I'm scared of what she's heard.

Dorcas is leaning against the sink for support and she looks shocked too.

I can't believe we've had a fight. The only friend I've ever really had.

'Please stop all the fighting.' Susan's voice is thin and reedy.

'It's OK, Susan. We've stopped. We aren't fighting. Don't worry about us.'

Susan is shaking like a shadow. 'She said you were The Witch.'

I flinch and try not to show how deeply it cuts.

'She said you wrote the curses.'

I don't say anything. It stings too much.

'It wasn't you. It was me.'

The room empties of air. Dorcas manages to make a word. 'What?'

'I'm The Witch.' Susan repeats herself. 'I am The Witch.'

I open and shut my mouth.

Dorcas can speak but only just. 'I don't understand.'

'I know it was wrong. It just got out of hand so quickly. I'm so sick of being invisible. No one ever notices me, and if they do it's to laugh at me, or poke fun at me. Poor little Susan Stevens, she hasn't got any friends. Poor little Susan Stevens she's *so* quiet, wouldn't say boo to a goose. On it goes, on and on. I'm nobody. I'm nothing. I just wanted to be noticed.'

She is the very opposite of me.

'I wanted everyone to know how it felt to hurt. I've seen everything. I know lots of things. I might not talk much, but I listen. At the start, I listened so I could try to make friends, but no one wanted to be friends with me. Day by day, I just got more invisible. Year by year, I disappeared. When the project started, I decided I wasn't going to be invisible anymore. I…'

She bursts into fresh tears.

'You are The Witch?' The first words I've managed.

'I am The Witch.'

We all turn to a noise behind us.

'Well, well, well. This just gets better and better.' Jemima has sidled in. 'The Witch has been discovered and now she must be tried.'

This is bad. This is very, very bad.

16

Jemima pushes Susan into a cubicle and traps her there while she waits for back up. 'We need to decide what to do with you, witch.'

This is awful. Terrible. Susan looks absolutely terrified.

'Leave her alone, Jemima.'

'Yes. Leave her alone.' Dorcas sounds stronger than me.

Jemima narrows her eyes in scorn.

'Or what? What are you going to do? Curse me again? Get your friend to write me a letter?' Her face is riddled with hate. An apple eaten by maggots.

'We need to give her a chance.' I attempt to push Jemima out of the way, but she's made of concrete obstinacy. 'When people are horrible, there are usually reasons. Like being overlooked for things.'

I glare at her so that she'll know I'm talking about her as well as Susan.

Jemima flinches but recovers in a milli-second. 'No reason is good enough.'

'Perhaps she wants to be noticed.' Again, I load what I say so Jemima will know I'm talking about her too, but it makes no difference. I hoped that Jemima would show some compassion because she has been hurt recently. She doesn't. She grabs Susan hard by the arm and drags her out of the toilets. Susan yowls.

We follow. As we get into the corridor, our class comes shrieking out on their way to the yard. This scuppers any hope I had of a teacher stepping in to stop this.

Jemima frog-marches Susan ahead and tells everyone to follow. They do. I get jostled out of the way, the other kids are so eager to keep up. People's yells crackle the corridors. Shoes march. The electric smell of fear and excitement. I look for the receptionist as we go past, but he isn't at his post. I can't wait for him. I have to stay with the others.

Susan is The Witch. I'm utterly gobsmacked. Quiet, unassuming Susan. She's the one who spread all that hate and malicious gossip. Maybe Susan deserves to be tried.

I catch the picture of Winter out of the corner of my eye. The people in it look wild, frenzied. Just like we are now. What am I thinking? What have I become? I'm so sorry. I need to stop this.

We are heading for the willow tree. I'm at the back of the crowd but the words pass through us like a snake from mouth to venomous mouth.

'Susan is The Witch.' I hear it over and over.

I can see Dorcas at the front, trying to wrestle with Jemima, but Jemima is strong, and everyone else is with her. They pull Dorcas away and she falls back into the pack. I wait. I don't know what to do.

We get to the willow too quickly. The green is a tangling cage today. It hides us from the outside world. Here there is no law except ours.

I'm torn. I want to run to get help. I want to stay to make sure things don't get any more out of hand.

'Quiet!' Everyone obeys Jemima immediately. Suspense fills the space. 'We have before us The Witch.'

I cower at the back as people hurl questions at

Susan. They are so angry. These curses burned away at us and kept us from sleeping night after night. The heat of them scorched us with humiliation, revealing secrets we were never going to tell.

I want to scream at them all to stop, but I'm afraid. Why should I put myself in danger? I haven't done anything.

Jemima holds her hand up.

'You want to know why she did it?'

A massive chorus of 'Yes'. The shoving is so hostile, I nearly get knocked over.

'Because she wanted a friend.'

There are jeers. Screeches.

Susan is held by Holly and one of the other girls. She's struggling to get free. 'Please,' she says, over and over. She is scared stiff. I have to help her.

'Stop this.' I push through. 'Stop this.'

I get to the front and look at them all. There's something in their faces I don't recognise. They've turned into a seething mass of rage.

Jemima holds her hand up again, but it takes a long time for her to get any hush this time. 'What do we have here? Another traitor?'

They surge forward. Branwen is toppled off her

feet. Lewis picks her up and takes her to the side, but even he is changed.

'I'm not a traitor. I just don't want this.' I can't think of the words. 'This is barbaric.'

Boos come at me full force.

'She was just lonely. She wanted to be noticed. We have to let her speak.'

'Let her speak,' Jemima says, and then, before anyone else can say anything, 'Let's give her a real trial.'

A roar of approval.

People begin arranging themselves. We've practised a witch trial often enough.

I close my eyes against the unfolding history of this place. This can't happen again. The birds are gathering. I can hear them even though no one else can.

Dorcas's hands swing helplessly at her sides. She looks at me. I can't give her anything.

Someone pushes me roughly from behind and I'm in my position as the executioner, whether I want to be or not.

Susan is shaking so much, it's amazing she's still upright. I want to put out my arm to help her, but I can't. I'm afraid. I'm afraid.

'Susan Stevens, you are brought before our court on this day under suspicion of witchcraft.' Jemima is enjoying her leading role at last. Her audience is rapt. 'You have put this class under your evil spell.'

All she's done is write some letters. Poisonous and spiteful letters, yes. Enchanted letters? Capable of cursing us? No.

We aren't the children of Year Six anymore, we are a court, a jury, a judge, an executioner.

'Why did you do this?'

'I was lonely. You don't know what it feels like to be lonely.'

I know exactly what she means. Loneliness is a killer.

'Lonely? Really? In fact, you wanted to – and I use your own words here – pay us all back, didn't you?' Jemima is milking the spotlight for all its worth.

'Yes. I felt like someone important for once. But it got out of hand and, once it started, I couldn't stop.'

'So, you do not deny that you are The Witch.'

'But…'

'A yes or no answer, please, Miss Stevens. Are you, or are you not The Witch?'

'Yes. But...'

The class gasp in astonishment as if they hadn't already heard this. Someone is casting an evil spell here, but it's not Susan.

The birds are getting so close.

'As you have no defence and no witnesses to speak on your behalf, may I suggest we bring this trial to an end with a guilty plea?'

I can't help myself. 'I'll be a witness for her.'

Even Jemima looks amazed. I don't know why I'm doing this. I should just shut up. Go along with the crowd.

'I've seen the way you all treat her. She's excluded from things. I didn't even notice her until she showed me the first curse note.' She wrote that first note. She showed me it for attention. 'It's not nice being lonely and alone. If you'd all treated her better, taken more notice of her, she wouldn't have done this.'

The birds zoom outside this swaying green light.

'So you are on her side?' Jemima's eyes are evil flames. I can't believe I made an effort to be kind to her. I've never wanted to punch someone so much in my whole life. She'll make every day hell for me for this. But what can she do? Term's nearly over. I'll move to another school. I'm not friends with Dorcas anymore anyway.

'I'm not on anyone's side. I just think you all could have been kinder. It wasn't nice to write those notes, at all, but she doesn't deserve this.'

'I think we'd better decide on Susan Stevens and then hold a second trial.'

This gets yells of approval. They're rattled by the thought that they may somehow be responsible. It was a wrong move to try to reason with them while they are in this state.

'First, let us decide on Susan's fate.'

'Guilty. Guilty.' Led by Jemima, they begin to chant.

'She is guilty!' Jemima raises her hands in the air triumphantly. 'She must be punished. How do we deal with witches, Year Six?'

They are going to start listing all the terrible things that have been done to witches. The hanging and drownings, burnings and executions. This is out of control. I'm going to get a teacher. I turn to leave.

'I'm not a witch,' Susan screams it so loud it stops me in my tracks. 'She is!'

I feel my neck prickle. I turn back slowly.

'She's been doing strange things ever since she got here.' Susan's voice is strangled but gaining momentum with each word. 'She communicates with birds.'

My head fizzes and burns.

'They follow her. You've seen it. You've all seen it.'

The birds are clouding the sky, their dark shadows clearly visible through the green. I clench my fists tight and hold them back.

I try to convince myself that no one really believes in witches here. Jemima is just a bully. Susan is just saying anything to get herself off the hook.

'She was in the toilets with Dorcas...'

The fury rushes through my veins like blood after a race. All the witches in history screech at me to escape. Run, they tell me. Run.

'...and Dorcas said she'd seen her flying.'

The birds are too strong now; there's no stopping them.

'Tell them, Dorcas.'

Dorcas never lies. She tries to say something, but Susan sees her loyalty and talks over the top of her. 'I'm not making it up. I'm not. Wilde's the real witch. It's her.'

She points her finger at me.

Everything is out of control. I'm running, with the whole class at my heels. Birds fly in my wake, fending off my classmates with beaks and claws. As soon as I run, the class see me for what I am. Though none of them really believe I can fly or that I'm a witch, they know now that I'm weird and weirdness is contagious. They want to deal with me once and for all.

17

I run all the way to the waterfall without thinking. I don't consider how treacherous the steps are or how I'll escape the gorge once I'm in it. My legs just take me there as if they've been programmed by someone else.

Some of the class are still close to me. The birds bought me a few minutes and some classmates gave up straight away but I can see Jemima and a few of the others are now gaining ground. If they'd follow me this far they must mean business. It's like they know where I'm going. Like something bigger than us is at work. My legs hurt from running but I can't stop and face them. I keep going against the pain.

Think clearly, Wilde. Don't panic. We have run away from school. It's Year Six code to keep things to ourselves but surely someone from our class will tell or one of the staff will notice.

I think of how empty the school is with most other classes on trips and residentials or working on their own end-of-term projects. The receptionist obsessed with his file and making calls. Gwyneth is preening and rehearsing and contacting her 'fans' on social media. No one will notice until it's too late.

I take the steps down two at a time, four at a time, ten at a time. At the bottom I crouch to recover. I don't know how I did that without breaking my ankles. Looking up, I can see the others through the trees. Jemima is shouting, howling, wild. There's no way out but up the steps I just came down. I look around desperately. I am too near the water. What are they going to do? They are out of control. I'll hide behind the waterfall. It's the only hope I have.

Scaling the rocks, I race along the path to the water. Not worrying about falling this time. Into that palace of glimmering light. It's too thin from the drought to hide me properly. I crouch in a corner. There is no escape.

They reach the bottom of the steps. *Please let them not see me. Please.*

Of course, they do. They know this place as

well as I do. Better. They've lived here all their lives. I press back into the rock. Water echoes. The world in falling patterns. Water spraying my face. I am part of this place. I will take them on.

I stand with my feet firmly on the floor, clench my fists, as they see me, and slip and slide along the path. Jemima leading. Dorcas. Holly. Susan. Lewis.

They face me, panting, tired. They look uncertain now. As if they know this has gone too far.

'Stop. This is madness.' I shout to be heard over the waterfall.

Susan looks wretched. Tears mark dirty lines down her face, and she is holding her stomach. I can see that she has been sick. I'm so angry for her. For me. For all the witches, and the ones who weren't but were punished anyway.

'This whole witch-hunt thing has got to stop,' I shout. 'You've been telling the story wrong for all these years. The legend of the witch, it's wrong.'

'Everything's gone wrong since you've been here.' Jemima isn't going to let it go. 'The curse has come back.'

She gets agreement from Holly and scared

silence from the others. Jemima shouts louder. 'It isn't just the letters. It's the real curse. Winter's curse is back, and it came back at the same time as you. Only this time you're trying to kill us with the heat. Soon there will be no water left and we'll die.'

'She hasn't brought the heat back. It's the climate crisis,' Dorcas shouts at Jemima and Jemima shoves her violently.

'Stop. Please stop it,' Susan begs.

The Falls of Snow thunder around us despite the lack of rain. We are in a different world here in this cave. Jemima shoves Dorcas again and she falls on to the path. I see blood on her face; she's hurt. Jemima kicks Dorcas while she's down.

'No!' I yell it louder than I've ever yelled before.

Jemima kicks Dorcas again and that's when I lose it. I can't hold the anger in anymore.

'No.' I throw my hands way above my head and make a noise I've never made before. 'Aeeeeeeeeeeyaaaaaaaaaeeeeeeeeeeeee'. High-pitched. Keening. It isn't human. It is Wilde's call. And they hear it.

The birds come crashing through the waterfall. My classmates scream and cower, but

I've gone too far to care. They deserve every bit of fear. I keen again, gutturally, then roar from deep in my belly. The sound fills the cavern. 'Yiiiiiiiiiiiiiiiiiiiiiaeeeeeeeyiiiii.'

I bring the birds to me in their hundreds. Let myself feel the magic properly for the first time. Channel the magic into them. The birds understand. I'm pouring the strength into them, and they grab the other children with their beaks and claws, lifting them through the curtain of water into the air. They take Dorcas. They take Susan and Lewis. Holly puts up a good fight but she's no match for them. Hundreds of birds of all kinds picking them up one by one. They try to take Jemima, but I grab her for myself, lift her into the air.

They all deserve this. They all betrayed me, like they all betrayed Winter. My anger is Arctic cold. Revenge for all the witches of history.

I step through the waterfall and hover. I'm not surprised to fly. It's as natural as the beating of my heart.

I hold Jemima high above the water.

They are all watching me now. These children, who think they can bully me, dangle in the air.

The drowning pool is below me. I see shapes in it. The seven sisters dancing. Winter emerging.

As she rises, everything becomes cold. The surface clouds into ice. The waterfall freezes into claws. Ice spreads out to the trees, making them white. Beautiful, sharp, glistening, fierce, bright white.

The birds shake the children like rag dolls. I can order them to release their puppets. Drop them and smash them all to smithereens.

Winter moves towards me. She is dressed in rags. Younger than I thought. About my age. I'm getting revenge for both of us. And for my mum.

The sky has turned black. Pictures move in the ice of the waterfall, dark, evil.

I am taking revenge for all of us.

Dorcas screams. 'No, Wilde. No.'

I get ready to tell the birds to smash their prey, but Winter smiles at me. I feel a shiver run through my body. I look into her face. I look at Jemima's face. Scared to death.

This is a crossroads. I can make a choice. I can kill everyone here and let witches hide forever, if there are any others out there. Or I can try to make these people understand. How it feels to be an outsider. What it feels like to be thought of as evil before you've even opened your mouth.

Enough of this. Winter was a good witch who turned bad because of the town's actions. I need everyone to hear her story. I won't turn bad because of pressure. I have choices. I can stop this. I land and set Jemima free. 'Enough.'

Winter disappears. The sky clears and the heat of the day returns. The ice melts and falls as water again from the waterfall. The surface of the pool cracks and the faces disappear. The children are let down gently by the birds, who swoop and sing.

Holly, Dorcas, Susan, Jemima and Lewis sit on the ground in shock.

I breathe in this beautiful place. I'm so sick of hiding. I'm not going to do it anymore. I am never going to hide again.

'I am a witch,' I shout to the hills and to them. 'I AM A WITCH.'

18

I yank down the colourful pictures and pull the feathers from the window of the treehouse. Kick the walls. Stamp on the cushions. Sink into a corner and bawl. I'm going to escape to the other side of the world today somehow. I was never meant to come here. It was always going to go wrong. That's why Dad always tried to stop me coming here. That's why Mae wouldn't tell me anything more about Mum. The magic is too strong for me to hide it when I'm here.

One of Dorcas's paintings has landed by my feet. I uncrumple it and then cry some more. I should have been stronger and kept my weirdness inside. It's all over now. I've ruined everything.

'Wilde.'

'What do you want?' I must have been crying too much to hear Dorcas arrive.

She doesn't say anything. She stays in the

doorway, then takes a step towards me, and immediately a step back.

'Oh dear, poor Dorcas. Afraid of me again, are you?'

The agony makes my words sharp. I squeeze myself further back into the corner. If anyone is afraid here, it's me.

Dorcas takes a tentative step inside and then another. Then she kneels down so she's on my level. The space between us has grown into a gulf and this time I can't fill it with kind words.

'Wilde. I…' She licks her lips nervously. 'I've never… We've never seen anything like that before. How is it even possible?'

I have an idea. My only hope. 'It was a trick. I've joined the magic circle. I've been practising and it was just a trick.'

The expression on Dorcas's face stops me. There's no point in pretending. I'm done with it.

'It wasn't a trick. I'm a witch.'

Dorcas doesn't run.

'I am but I don't want to be. I want to be normal like everyone else, but I'm a witch. Always have been. Always will be.'

She doesn't respond.

'My mother was a witch. Her mother was a witch before her. The witch called Winter was one of my ancestors. That's why strange things have been happening since I've been here. Weird stuff follows me around. Birds, yes. But there have been more here than anywhere else. I think it's because I am close to where my family came from. I think Winter has been trying to talk to me somehow. The story about her, it's not what happened. My mother has been trying to communicate with me, too, I think.'

I smooth out Dorcas's painting and prop it up against the wall while I muster the energy to continue.

'The flying is a new thing to me. I didn't lie to you about that. I just didn't believe it. Also seeing things in mirrors, glass, water. It's called scrying. That's never happened to me before either. That was my mother's gift.'

Dorcas is dumbfounded. I'm not surprised. I would be too. I go to speak again but she holds up her hand and I wait, listening to the sounds of summer outside and the hard, low thud of my heart.

'Firstly, that's the most you've spoken in one go ever.' Her voice is shaky.

'I'm trying to be more like you.' It's a poor effort at a joke, and Dorcas stops me again.

'Secondly, I don't understand. Witches don't exist, do they? Really? I mean people were accused of witchcraft, but it wasn't real?'

'It is real. I've had to hide it all my life. I lost my temper. I just couldn't keep it in anymore.'

'So if you lose your temper again?'

'I've always managed to control it. The birds. I got them to put you all down, didn't I?' This is difficult. I can feel the anger starting to gather and the birds coming towards us. I will them away hard and push my feelings back down deep.

'I don't know, Wilde. The others are pretty scared. None of them want to come anywhere near you.'

That stings so sharply I can't swallow.

'What if you can't control it? When you're angry again.'

'I can.' I shift uncomfortably.

'But what if you can't?'

There is an endless silence while I realise how hopeless this all is.

'Are there more of you? Witches?'

'I don't know. I've never met any.' The crack in

my voice stops me for a second. 'I don't know. I've always been hiding. Perhaps, if there are others, they are doing the same.' I swallow hard again. 'Or perhaps I am the only one.'

Dorcas looks out of the window when I say that. She was my first real, proper friend.

'I'm lonely, Dorcas.' Those three words fill the world. 'I'm all alone.'

She stands. I do the same. I search her face for clues.

'I'm going to go now.'

I don't want her to feel bad. It's not her fault.

'Don't worry about it, Dorcas.'

She doesn't reply. Just leaves the treehouse with her head down. My first ever true friend found out what I am and now she is gone. I smooth the rest of her pictures and lay them flat so she can collect them from Mae. Tidy the cushions so they won't get broken. Straighten the Crow's Nest sign by the door on my way out.

When I get to the bottom of the ladder, Dorcas is there waiting. It's now or never. I need to do this before my chance is gone.

'Dorcas, I need to tell you the story of what really happened to the witch called Winter.'

19

They all hate me now. I know they do. I don't want to talk to anyone ever again.

I'll just take my important things and leave the rest. Dad will just have to come back this time. I'll go back to our yellow flat by the sea and get the emergency key from Sam next door. I can get a train to Swansea and then a bus along the sea front to Mumbles. It's fine. I'll let Mae know when I get there. I don't want to worry her with my problems when her business is struggling and she's so stressed out.

I pack in my bedroom. I've brought my stuff in from the treehouse. Mae's out somewhere. I wrap my seagull skull in tissue paper. I'll fix it when I get home.

Birds have always been important to me. There was the nightingale that sang me to sleep when I was little; the robin who came to my windowsill at my last school; and the jackdaws, owls, jays, starlings, kites and crows who are always around. They are my protectors.

'Sorry, Mum. I tried.' I put her photo inside the Shakespeare book next to one of her favourite sonnets and zip my new backpack up.

I push a squeaky floorboard with my toe to hear it protest for the last time and smooth the glass of the mirror, wondering if the shadows inside can see me as I can see them.

'Goodbye, room.' I stop in the doorway. 'And thank you.'

There's a noise outside. A loud noise. People. The mob. I drop my case, not even thinking about the clasp, and look out.

The whole town. All the children and adults are coming for me. I can't escape. They are pouring into the garden. Blocking all the exits. I look at the skylight. I don't want to, but I'll go that way if I have to.

'Wilde!'

I turn. Ready to fight.

'What on earth is the matter with you? I've been looking for you everywhere.'

The witch window is behind me and I can fly

sideways to get out if I need to. Any witch could. I know who I am now and what powers I have.

'What is it, Wilde? You are white as a sheet.'

'My sheets are blue.'

'It's a saying. But, actually, it doesn't make sense, does it?'

'Nothing makes sense.' I can hear the mob behind me. They are shouting and laughing. Laughing? I'll make them laugh on the other side of their faces.

'They've moved your class play to our garden. The temperature in the school hall is too high and the classrooms are filled with birds. There are birds everywhere. It's the heat, driven them mad. They won't let people get in.'

I don't know what to do. I can't seem to move.

'Come on, Wilde. Snap out of it. Something tells me this was meant to be, that's why I'm allowing it. Also, I don't want your project to be spoiled even if it is about witches.'

I am frozen to the spot.

'We need to get cracking because there's a storm forecast and you know how people feel about lightning here. I've told them they can use the garden as long as I can have a hand in running their next project. They've agreed. The garden is going to be a theatre again! Isn't that wonderful?' Mae jumps up and down with excitement.

I look out of the window. People are spreading blankets on the grass and sitting down. Unpacking picnics. Patting the animals. Smelling the flowers. Eating sandwiches and chatting. A couple have brought wishful raincoats and are staring hopefully at the sky. It feels like the whole town is there, but they don't look vicious. They've come for a celebration.

My class are all crowded around the tree discussing something. I bet it's me. They'll wait until they have everyone's attention and then they'll tell the whole audience what I am. Right there, where my mum stood. In my garden.

Right. I'll play their game and, when the moment comes, I'll show them just what a witch can do.

'I'll come down with you now.' I push my case closer to the door, where I can collect it easily when I need to, and follow Mae downstairs. She chit-chats the whole way but I don't listen. I plan how I will teach them a lesson. How dare they come here into my mum's theatre to get revenge against me? How dare they?

When I get into the garden, dark clouds have begun to gather on the horizon. The audience are oblivious. All smiles and anticipation. They'll get a show alright.

Jemima comes towards me and I stand my ground.

She says, 'We've changed the casting. You have to play the role of Winter because you are a witch.' She grabs my wrist and drags me towards the stage. I shake myself free and am glad when she's too afraid to try to snatch me again. I will go on the stage and give everyone a spectacle they will never forget.

Gwyneth Fox-Rutherford sits in a chair with DIRECTOR written on it in large letters right at the front. She has a bandage on her foot.

'Turns out I broke a bone. I fear the play will be much less effective without my brilliance treading the boards, but you and the others shall have to overcome. The show must go on, after all.'

I will play a condemned witch. How ironic. I feel the birds stretch their wings in preparation. They have brought people here for a reason. High in the hills they wait. Circling the windmill, soaring above the Falls of Snow, bringing the darkness with them, they wait. I'll play the role of Winter, but this time the witch won't be going to the gallows.

I look at the others as I make my way to the stage, but not one of them dares to meet my eye. The fairy lights twinkle and star the boughs and the windows of the treehouse. In other circumstances this would be beautiful. Not now.

I stand centre stage, in Winter's spot, as the story begins to unfold around me. I stare straight out at the people of this town. The ones whose ancestors turned on Winter. The ones whose forefathers condemned her.

The woman who gives me extra grated cheese at lunch in Witch Point Primary is bouncing a baby on her knee. Mr Ricketts is standing at the back so he can get a really good view. He is trying to flatten his quiff and laughing, so I know he can't be ill anymore. Mae and Jules are standing at the side, putting their thumbs up to me and patting Denzel the dog. Mrs Danvers has her own seat in the front row. Year Five are here on blankets and deckchairs. The other classes are making faces at my class.

'This is the story of the witch called Winter.' I'm astounded to see Susan taking the opening line. 'She was a terrible witch. A hideous hag who cast a horrible spell to disguise herself.'

'This is the story of how she came into our home and tricked us all.' Holly's voice rings out clear and loud against the excited hubbub.

'She decided to come into my house and steal my seven daughters away.' Lewis brandishes his axe high above his head like a warrior.

The executioner comes towards me and takes down their hood. It's Jemima, of course.

'No.' I say it quietly the first time. 'No.'

'Only this time the story is going to be told in a different way.' Jemima's voice shakes with nerves. I am confused.

Dorcas walks forward and stands on the other side of me.

'It's time to put the story right. To put everything right.'

Susan hands me a note. I open it with trembling hands and read to myself.

'We, the undersigned, have agreed to give you a chance. Not because we couldn't have you locked up

198

forever for what you did to us at the waterfall, because we could, (especially if I was the lawyer – Jemima) but because Dorcas told us what really happened to Winter and we think the truth should be told. We don't like it when things are unfair even if they happened a long time ago. The rest of the class don't know what you are, or why we are changing things, but Jemima has told them she's annoyed she didn't get a main part and to improvise as we go along.

If you lift the curse, we will never tell what happened because it is Year Six code. We will never tell our other classmates (not even Ivy – Holly). We will never tell anyone. The choice is yours.

Jemima. Dorcas. Susan. Lewis. Holly.

P.S. I don't think anyone would believe what happened even if we did tell them – Dorcas.

P.P.S. I really am annoyed I didn't get a main part – Jemima.

P.P.P.S. Please don't kill us – Lewis.

Everyone looks at me. I find my voice. It's strong.

'This is the real story of what happened to the witch called Winter.'

20

'There have been too many witch hunts in Witch Point.'

I don't like being on a stage, but this story needs me to tell it.

'One of the most famous was the witch called Winter.'

Maybe this is a trap of some kind, but I am going to tell this story if it's the last thing I ever do.

'There was a cottage in the woods.'

The others all run to the side of the stage and leave me alone. I dig deep inside and find the courage to continue.

'An orphan girl found herself in the cold forest, alone and without food.'

Dorcas comes back on holding the elaborate moon on a stick from the *Midsummer Night's Dream* costumes which we found in the attic. She shines a torch at it so it gleams.

'Finding a cottage in the woods, she asked them to give her some scraps.'

Lewis comes on holding his axe and the cardboard wall from the attic. Mae must have let them have all the props she and my mum made.

'Because the girl was so grateful to the woodcutter and his wife for taking her in, she did everything she could to help them and their seven daughters.'

Some of the class hold up golden wands so they look like stars. Some shine lights on the flimsy stars which were hanging in the attic and now hang from the tree.

'Soon after she arrived, the seven sisters became jealous because she was getting attention from their parents. Also, Winter was gifted. She could grow flowers anywhere.'

Jemima starts singing and signals to the rest of the class. The others rush on and fill the stage with the flowers that have been saved at the back of the house. It's so beautiful I can feel my lip quiver, but I have to concentrate. I'm starting to believe that they might be on my side.

'She could calm fierce animals, tell the future in water, birds came to her wherever she went. The kinder Winter was, the more the sisters grew jealous.'

One of the girls comes in wearing a lion mask and Cai comes on wearing the donkey's head from *A Midsummer Night's Dream*. He's can't see where he's going because the ears are so far over the eyeholes and someone leads him across to meet Duran Duran, the real donkey. This gets loads of laughs from the audience. And a smile from me.

'Winter had been to many places and brought stories of the outside. The seven sisters had never been anywhere, and they wanted to escape. The sisters hatched a plan. If their parents loved Winter so much, they could have her to themselves. They would go and leave her behind.'

The clouds are knitting themselves thicker in the sky. My voice is clear. I will get to the end of this story and then tell the whole town that I am a witch too. I can do this.

'One day, snow began to fall.' I look up to see Lewis shaking pieces of confetti over me. He waves and the confetti wobbles and spills a bit. 'Winter, who loved nature and the beauty of snow, called them out to see the intricate patterns of the snowflakes. This suited their plan perfectly. They had stored some supplies behind the Falls of Snow waterfall and they led Winter there.'

Jemima directs the class with more gestures. We are so used to improvising now. They move to sit and listen at the side of the stage. Gwyneth looks baffled but interested. Elvis the duck sits on her lap as if he's preventing her from moving.

'When they arrived, they told her they were going to leave. She tried to stop them, and they fought. Overpowering her, because there were seven of them, they tied her up and left her behind the waterfall. As they left, the waterfall froze over, leaving her trapped by a cage of ice. One of the sisters, who wasn't quite as bad as the others, left her some food.'

I think of the drawing of the cage my mum drew. A sudden soft wind whispers through the ribbons and garlands and makes them ripple like a waterfall. I swallow hard. I'm nearly there. I've nearly told it all.

'Winter stayed there with her hands tied for three days and nights before the waterfall thawed enough for the birds to get through. They untied her ropes with their beaks.'

Actual birds start to land on the fences and the house. It's so magical having them there watching. They have protected me and my ancestors. I am telling the story for them as well.

'Winter made her way back to the woodcutter's house and told the woodcutter and his wife what had happened. They wouldn't believe her because, of course, they couldn't believe that of their seven daughters.'

The day has become so dark and hot that the solar lamps around the house turn on. I wipe sweat from my upper lip. Everyone is listening.

'They took her to the town and the woodcutter and his wife told the people of Winter's gifts. All the people blamed her for the disappearance of the seven sisters. The poor girl went to trial and the town condemned her as a witch.'

The class all turn their backs on me as we've rehearsed for Gwyneth's version of the play and I stand at the gallows, imagining the fear that Winter must have felt. The terror coursing through her veins, crystallizing into hate when no one listened.

'She was hanged as a witch and, in desperation, just before she died, she cursed the town until the truth be told. And now you look on me. Wilde. At the gallows. And when you know how weird I am, you will condemn me too.'

I have to do this. To show them who I really am. I'm so sick of hiding. Sick to my bones. 'I am a witch. I can call the birds to me. I can fly.'

I should fly to show them, but I'm so tired. Looking at these people, this town where I was meant to grow up, I can't summon the power. I stand at the gallows, broken, exhausted, wanting to be accepted, wanting to sleep without fear.

Jemima comes towards me as the hangman. She turns to the audience and I wait for whatever cruelty she has planned. Perhaps her nastiness will give me energy again.

She projects loudly, 'I am a witch too.'

I gasp.

'I am so weird I can pop the cork from a bottle with my voice.'

She takes a bottle from one of the others and puts it down in front of her. She then puts her fingers in her ears and sings the highest note any human has ever hit. The cork pops out of the bottle and there is a stunned silence followed by rapturous applause and cheers from the audience.

'I am a witch too.' Dorcas steps forward. 'I breathed life back into a spider once. It was in the shower and I didn't notice, and it was almost washed down the plughole and I took it out on toilet roll and blew on it gently until it came back to life.'

She gets a round of applause. With my love of spiders, I bite back tears.

'I'm a witch. I'm so weird I can recite the alphabet backwards!' Lewis only gets as far as 'S' but gets a huge cheer anyway and jumps offstage to start signing autographs straight away.

'We are witches. We can do this!' Ivy pretends to be a ventriloquist's dummy for Holly. It's so realistic, it's actually quite scary.

The others join in. Branwen can make her eyebrows dance and Cadi has broccoli for breakfast, which doesn't prove she is a witch but certainly is weird. Thomas, Cai and some of the other boys hang by their legs from the trees and then somersault down. Mabli goes *en pointe* without shoes for more than ten seconds, which is miraculous.

Susan Stevens steps forward. 'I am a witch.' She looks to me for encouragement. I nod and smile, though there are tears spilling down my cheeks. 'I am a witch and so weird I can do this…'

She picks up one of the candles Mae hasn't let us light and passes her hand over the top of it. The wick flickers into flame. I wonder if I am the only descendant of Winter here.

When they have all announced their witchery, the class all turn to me. They are all so brilliantly weird. We are all so brilliantly weird in our own ways. Those who now know what I really am and those that don't.

'We are all witches because we are all magic.' My voice is trembling, but I will never be silent again, even if I am afraid. 'We are all weird. So, instead of fighting it, let's celebrate our weirdness?'

I ask it as a question and the audience murmurs its agreement. There is a rumble of thunder and everyone looks up.

'You haven't shown us what you can do, Wilde,' Dorcas says loudly, then turns her back to the audience and whispers to me, 'Make it look like a trick.'

This is *the* moment, *my* moment. 'I am a witch and I can fly.'

I float up, just a little, staying low enough for it to look like an illusion, a trick of the eye. But I am flying. I am myself.

I feel something strange on my face. An unfamiliar but so familiar feeling. I realise what it is and throw my hands up into the air and laugh.

'Oh, and also, I can make it rain!'

This gets a standing ovation and a cheer as the rain begins to fall faster.

'That wasn't you really, was it?' Dorcas's curls twinkle with raindrops and the shine of the garden's lights.

'Of course it wasn't. I'm not that powerful.'

'Shame.' Jemima stands next to me. 'Is the curse gone?'

I wonder if the storm was purely coincidence or if it was Winter sending us a message. I take a deep breath of air. It smells different. Sweeter. Something beyond the heavenly fragrance of freshly falling rain. I nod. I really think it is.

'Truce then. As long as you never ever do anything bad to me again.'

'I won't. I'm so sorry, Jemima. But, likewise, you have to stop being such a bully.'

'I'm not a bully.'

I look at Jemima and raise my eyebrows in mock disbelief.

'Oh alright. I'll try a bit, as long as things go my way. Also, Mae tells me she is setting up a theatre company with you?'

It's the first I've heard of it but, looking around me, I wonder if perhaps it would be quite fun. As long as we don't do plays about witches. I look at Jemima and I know that if we do, of course she'll be cast in our plays because she is the best actress of all of us.

'Yes. I really want to. I've been planning it for ages.' For once, the lie doesn't hurt.

'Awesome news.' She grabs Holly and pulls her over to us. 'Holly won't tell anyone either, will you?'

Holly moves in closer. 'I've never ever kept a secret from Ivy before. I so want to have a secret of my own and this one is just brilliant.' Her eyes glow mischievously. 'Is that bad?'

'In this case, no.' Dorcas smiles.

Jemima swings her hair and slaps me in the face with her ponytail. Not a completely reformed character yet then.

Lewis is still signing people's programmes and

arms, but he looks up and grins. I'm so glad to have stuck up for him when the chips were down. I know in my heart I can trust him. I watch as he picks up his baby brother and laugh when his brother is sick all over his shoulder. Lewis laughs too. I guess the grossness of baby sick is something you get immune to.

Dorcas links her arm through mine. 'Thank you, Wilde.'

'What for?'

'Being so totally odd. The best thing that has ever happened to us bunch of misfits at Witch Point Primary is to know a real witch. It's really, truly, brilliantly weird.'

I laugh, then cry Wilde's call to the birds.

'Aeeeeeeeeeeyaaaaaaaaaeeeeeeeeeeeee'.

They fly up and break the clouds as shimmering rain pours down harder. Mae puts some music on and plays it loudly from the porch. People dance, laugh, shelter, show each other their own weird abilities.

Dorcas hugs me, then we jump up and down in the weirdest way we can, splashing water up from the puddles which are appearing everywhere. Holly throws herself in to join the bouncing group hug. Jemima walks away then changes her mind and dives at us. We hoot with laughter and keep jumping.

From the corner of my eye, I see Susan walking towards the garden gate.

'I'll be right back. Keep jumping!'

I dash through the rain, bumping into dancing people. 'Susan, wait.'

She is at the gate now, and I worry she won't hear me over the noise of the party behind, but she stops.

'You aren't going anywhere.' I think of the magic she just did. Lighting a flame from nothing. Perhaps, just perhaps it was real magic. I could ask her about it, but I know how personal a decision it is to say. She will tell me if she wants to.

'You need to join the party. You have to make an effort. You have to put yourself out there.'

'But what I did to you. Accusing you like that. It was awful. I was so scared.'

I know what fear looks like. Perhaps facing that fear was the only way to let out who I truly am. 'You did me a favour, in a really strange way.'

'But I'm sorry. I'm so sorry, Wilde.'

'You should be.'

She stares at me with pain in her eyes and I stare back with the rain plastering my hair to my head and the whooping and chaos behind me. Susan needs to be a part of this happiness. We all do.

Grabbing her by the hand we run back into the garden and jump higher than anyone else.

21

'Yeah,' Tom Jones says as I leave the house.

The sky is freshly washed. The clouds are white and puffy, hung out to dry in the startling blue. It's the start of the holidays and it's going to be good. I can't stop smiling. My cheeks ache. I think I must have smiled through a whole night's peaceful sleep.

The curse has been lifted. The streets are empty. Birds hop about happily in the puddles and in the glistening trees. I check that my raven brooch is attached to my T-shirt. I don't need to get it fixed to wear it proudly. It was my mum's and it has history.

'Dad.' It's gone through to his voicemail. 'Dad. I'll see you later, but I wanted you to know. I'm happy to stay here. I want to stay here.'

He is away working lots and there's plenty of room here. We can use our yellow flat by the sea for holidays and weekends. It's not so far away. I'm hoping to talk him into it tonight when he gets back. Something tells me he won't need much persuading when he sees how happy I am. I'll tell him about the plans we have to start our garden theatre company. I'm still going to travel the world one day but first it's time for a new story here.

I have one more message to deliver before I can start afresh. I type it into my phone, choosing my words carefully and honestly.

'Dear Wilde.

A letter to yourself. I just wanted you to remember that you are changing your ways. Perhaps, one day, you'll be able to tell everyone the story of who you really are and why you caused so much trouble. Until then I want you to know that you are doing your best and life isn't easy. I hope you will forgive yourself and if you sometimes worry that you aren't doing brilliantly, remember life is easier with friends, but you managed on your own for a long time and you can do that again, because inside you there is a good person who tries really hard. Alone doesn't always mean lonely. The most important thing is being a friend with yourself.

Yours hopefully, Wilde.'

I save it and take a deep breath. It's cooler today after the rain. The air feels different. Clean and without a trace of curse. I like it here in my new life. I like Witch Point a lot.

Dorcas and Susan are meeting me at the waterfall. We are calling ourselves the three weird sisters and we are going swimming.

Acknowledgements

On my travels I have met so many extraordinary young people. You have made me remember how much courage it takes to be young, so my first big thank you goes to you. Without you my stories would be nothing. You create the magic.

Thanks to my brilliant editor Janet Thomas, who has again worked her dazzling enchantments on my words, and my gorgeous agent Kate Shaw, who stirred the spell of belief in my stories when my self-belief was at the bottom of a very murky cauldron. Thanks to Meg, Simone, Penny, and Rebecca of Firefly Press for making the book fly without a broomstick and to Anne Glenn for making it sparkle like the most beautiful of spells. You are wonderful witches, all.

My coven of friends who have stuck by me through all sorts of bad luck charms. Special thanks to fellow writers Janine Barnett-Phillips, Rhian Ivory, Jennifer Killick and Jane Fraser, who have cheered me on from afar on an almost daily basis.

Thanks to all the teachers, librarians, booksellers, bloggers and vloggers who have cast my stories further than I ever imagined possible. Thanks to Literature Wales and Books Council Wales, who have supported me from when I was a mere witchling.

Wilde, Dorcas and I would like to thank Robin Stevens for creating the *Murder Most Unladylike* Mysteries. We are huge fans of Daisy Wells and Hazel Wong and wish that our detecting skills were as good as theirs.

My husband Guy, who must have swallowed about a thousand patience potions while I wrote *Wilde*.

My familiar Watson Jones, super-dog and chief pitchfork waver.

My sister Jo, who once threw me down the stairs in a sleeping-bag and taught me resilience.

My mum and dad, for the costumes, the turnip lanterns and the years of stories.

My niece Rosie, who will teenage eye-roll when she sees this but will immediately check to make sure she's been mentioned before said eye-rolling commences.

The rest of my family, who taught me who I am and how to be an individual. This is a story about individuality. I lost my Aunty Carol to diabetes on 24th November 2019. The world will never be the same without her. She was a true individual and she taught me a lot.

To all the characters in books who were for a long time my only friends. Thank you.

Thanks to all the fellow witches in the world. You are brave, you are beautiful, you are Wilde.